Al

SUNDAY'S CHILD
HITLER'S JUDAS
(Books one and two of the Pea Island Gold trilogy)

MY KING THE PRESIDENT

(Coming soon :)

LUCIFER'S CHILDREN
ZENA'S LAW

In memory of

J.T. and Carolyn

And for my three siblings,

Georgia, Diane, and Linda

Sons of Their Fathers

Prologue

New York, October 3, 1978

Thunderous bravos, several curtain calls, and three encores—what every performing artist prays for. Works for. Lives for. The knowledgeable Town Hall audience responded to Dieter Bach's third recital there with all three, and Dieter was on a euphoric high when he carefully packed his Guadanini, then opened his dressing room door. At the head of the line waiting to congratulate him was his rotund manager, Sy Glazer, beaming from ear to ear. Before Dieter began shaking hands and signing autographs, Sy whispered, "Your best one yet, Dieter. Hurry up with this stuff and let's go somewhere and celebrate."

Dieter smiled at him. He knew that Sy meant 'Hurry up, I'm getting hungry.' Nevertheless, his chubby manager was accurate about this performance. It *had* been his best. Had showed the most maturity. A small personal triumph, too, since the Brahms sonata had gone especially well.

Within an hour, they were in a taxi, headed for the Stage Deli. Sy's idea of every post-concert celebration was a huge meal-- no matter what the time of day or night. And, as usual, Sy ate enough for both of them, chattering the whole time. Dieter believed it was Sy's intention to sit there eating and drinking until the morning papers--and reviews--came out. After an hour or so, Dieter left him there and took a taxi back to the Mayflower, thinking he might now have calmed down enough to sleep.

Dieter loved the Mayflower. Besides its proximity to important spots in Manhattan, he loved its old-fashioned rooms and service, its brown walls and frayed carpets, so much like a once grand lady caught out in an old dress and without fresh makeup. He got out of the taxi and glanced at his watch, noting it was nearly two in the morning. The October air was cool, but not unpleasant, and on impulse, he decided he wasn't ready yet to go inside. He was still what Sy called 'wired', and needed a walk.

He crossed the street, unmindful there was no traffic at all, and started walking south, by the park's wall, his brain replaying the last movement of the Brahms, which, until tonight's performance, had always been a little troublesome. He didn't notice the three men until they pushed him up against the wall, demanding money. His wallet. Even then, Dieter didn't think about danger. Or death. He was still 'on stage'. He didn't see the short-barreled pistol pointed at him. He heard none of the profane shouting. Nothing of reality registered until one of the three black men tried to take his violin.

He would gladly have given those men his wallet if he'd had one, or anything else. But not the violin. Not his

Guad. And when they tried to take it, he resisted. Clasped it to his chest, holding it tight with both gloved hands. Only when the two shots came, obliterating the Brahms passage, did he see death. Face on. Then he felt it. The canvas-covered wooden case suddenly banged against his chest, very hard. Hard enough to knock him to the sidewalk, his topcoat bunched up around his waist. Even then he didn't realize he had been shot. His mind recorded a vague picture; a slow-motion black and white film of his attackers running away, and he was barely conscious of crawling to the front door of the hotel and reaching the lobby before fainting.

But he still had his violin.

He still clutched his precious Guadanini, a rare violin which would never sound another tone. Nor would Dieter Bach ever produce another note on any other violin.

Bonn, West Germany, October 4, 1978

The policeman's office reflected the man himself. Neat. Orderly. Not a single item on his large steel desk, or in the six matching filing cabinets was out of place. The fresh-waxed floor shone like the baked paint of a new car. One small Venetian-blinded window offered a slanted view of the third floor façade of an equally drab sister building no more than ten meters away. There were no photographs, pictures, or any other decorative appurtenances gracing the other three pale green walls—with the exception of appropriately framed diplomas and award certificates accumulated over the years. They all hung behind him in positions perfectly spaced between each other, the ceiling, and at eye level for anyone sitting in either of the two formal straight-backed chairs facing his desk. His own chair was no less rigid; its only sop to comfort was a thin, form-fitting cushion which the policeman didn't really need. The only reason he used it was because his mother had made it for him and given it to him for his birthday five years ago.

The policeman was not a doodler. He had never been seen reading a newspaper or working crossword puzzles in his sanctuary. In fact, neither his secretary nor either of his two subordinates ever saw anything on top of his desk other than the large calendar, the two telephones (one black, one orange), whichever bound file he was working on, and a small photograph of his mother, ensconced in an ornate silver frame.

Often, the policeman could be seen sitting quite still, hardly breathing, almost as if frozen, his eyes mere slits. At such times, his people knew not to disturb him; he was thinking through a problem. He was in such a mode now. Waiting. Waiting for a specific telephone call. When the orange phone finally rang, he allowed himself a slight smile. "Yes?"

"I have located him."

"Are you certain it's him?"

"Quite certain."

"Good work. Where?"

"It is complicated. How soon can you meet me in Buenos Aires?"

"Tomorrow. Call me back in thirty minutes. I will let you know the flight number and arrival time."

"All right. You'll bring the money?"

"Of course."

"I'll call back in thirty minutes exactly."

The policeman hung up the phone, his smile a little wider. He took one satisfying stretch before leaning forward to open the thick file in front of him. One he had added to for many, many years.

He hadn't been at it for more than two minutes when the black phone rang. Slightly irritated, he picked it up. "Yes?"

"This is Johnny. I'm calling from New York."

"Why? Has the status of the subject changed?"

"Well, yes, you could say that. He's been shot."

The policeman sat up. Alarmed. "Dead?"

"No, but he is in the hospital. I don't know how serious his condition is."

"Find out and call me back in three days."

"Yes, sir. Anything else?"

"No. Goodbye."

The policeman rang off, and then punched the intercom for his secretary. "Book me on the first available flight to Buenos Aires."

The secretary knew better than to ask why. "Right away, sir. First class?"

"It doesn't matter."

"Will you be taking the brown suitcase or the black one?"

The brown one. "I'll be back day after tomorrow."

"Very good, sir."

The policeman frowned as he replaced the phone. Bad news invariably followed good. Such was his life. Had been for as long as he could remember, and he could remember in detail as far back as when he was three years old. By the age of four, he had already begun practicing the patience it took to deal with it.

He bent forward again to the file. One day, perhaps soon, this file would finally be closed.

◆

Chapter 1

Two of New York's tired and overworked finest, Detectives Joe Carmody and his partner, Abe Farkas, walked into room 419 at Mercy. An equally exhausted doctor standing by the bed with his arms crossed turned and gave the two cops a scowl, then moved aside for them. "You can have ten minutes. He's still pretty woozy from his medication."

Carmody nodded, his eyes moving from the young emergency room doctor to the man lying on the bed; both hands elevated and wrapped in serious bandages. "Don't worry, Doc, this won't take long. "Uh, how you feeling, Mr. Bach? Up to answering a few questions?"

Dieter answered, "I can try. Are you the Police?"

"That's right. My name's Carmody. NYPD. This is my partner, Detective Farkas. Your case was assigned to us." While talking, Carmody had removed a pad from his pocket. He flicked the nub of his ballpoint. "Listen, can you give us a description of the three punks who jumped you?"

Dieter shook his head slowly. "I can't tell you what they looked like, except that they were all black men."

Farkas asked, "Were they tall? Short? Thin? Fat? Do you remember anything they might have said? Any of them call out names?"

"I'm sorry, I don't remember. It was dark. I didn't really see...They were all three yelling at me. I think they were all wearing coats and hats—no, not hats, those caps with a... with a-"

"A bill?" Farkas helped. "Like baseball caps?"

"Yes, I think so. Baseball hats."

Farkas and Carmody exchanged quick glances. Carmody said, "Yankees? Mets? Red Sox?"

Dieter lowered his eyes. Bit his lip. "I... I don't know. I don't follow baseball."

Carmody sighed. They were not going to get much help from this vic. Typical. "I understand, Mr. Bach. We're gonna do our best to catch 'em, though. You weren't carrying a billfold. Lucky for us the Mayflower people ID'd you."

What Carmody didn't say was, *"If you had, you might not be here. Those sonsabitches were probably looking for a couple bucks to buy a fix."*

"I had just finished playing a concert. I had left my wallet in my hotel room, I didn't need...think I needed..."

"It's okay, sir," Farkas said, realizing the poor guy was embarrassed as hell that he couldn't be more helpful. "Hey, I wanna show you something." He fished in his pocket and held up a small metal object about the size of a flat-sided bean. "We got one little clue, anyway. This is the bullet that hit you. Looks like a 32 slug. Ballistics will tell us for sure. We found it where you were lying on the floor of the lobby, underneath your overcoat."

Dieter stared hard at the thing. It didn't look like a bullet. More like a lead fishing weight a boy might have pounded with a hammer. "I don't understand."

Carmody turned to the doctor. "You wanna help us out, here, Doc?"

Doctor Vincent Taliaferro took a couple steps forward. Leaned over Dieter's bed. "You were apparently holding your violin against your chest with both hands; the right one overlapping the left. One bullet passed through both your hands first, which slowed it down some, then it passed through your violin case, which flattened it out and slowed it down a lot more. It finally slammed into your chest; actually your, ah, breastbone. It must have lodged in your clothing and come loose when you crawled back to the hotel."

Slow recognition dawned on Dieter's face. "Wait, you said it passed through my violin case? My *violin?*"

"That's right," Carmody said. That violin and its wooden case saved your life, Mr. Bach. Was it real valuable?"

Still mentally struggling under the influence of the pain killing drugs, Dieter nonetheless understood the man had said 'was,' not 'is'. "It was extremely valuable."

"Well," Carmody said, sympathetically, "I'm sure you had it insured. Tell you what, though, hadn't been for that violin and the case it was in, you'd be lying in the morgue right now."

Dieter nodded. Tears came which he couldn't wipe away. His voice dropped to a whisper. "Where is it? I want to see it."

Another quick glance passed between the two detectives. "You sure?" Farkas asked.

"Yes. Please."

Farkas shrugged, went back through the door, and reappeared a few moments later carrying Dieter's most prized possession. He held it up, showing Dieter the small round holes where the bullets went in, then turned it over, revealing the splintered gashes where they had exited. "We didn't find the second bullet," Farkas said.

Copious tears now flowed freely down Dieter's cheeks. "Open it, please."

Again, the detective looked at the young physician for help. Farkas handed him the case. "You're the one with the good hands, Doc. You do it."

Dieter watched as Doctor Taliaferro unzipped the brown canvas case, unsnapped the latches, and reverently opened it, like opening a casket. Inside laid the mangled corpse of the Guadanini. Dieter blinked several times, not quite believing. He was also unaware of reverting back to his native tongue with his nearly inaudible vocal reaction, *"Mein Gott!"* Now in pain worse than from his hands, he squeezed his eyes shut. He didn't see the well-meaning doctor carefully place the closed case on the window sill, nor did he hear the few remaining questions the two detectives had before adding their condolences and departing, shaking their heads and promising to do their best. They knew, from hard experience, that there was probably less than a slim chance of ever apprehending the three muggers. If they did, considering their already humongous case load, they'd have to get luckier than Dieter Bach had been unlucky.

Left alone with his patient, Doctor Taliaferro was thinking other thoughts. He knew that while losing an expensive, possibly irreplaceable instrument was nasty medicine for a professional musician to take, Dieter Bach had a much more serious problem. In fact, two. The x-rays had made the complete sequence of events fairly obvious. It was the first shot that had done the damage. The bullet had gone through the leather of Dieter's right hand glove, passed through his right hand squarely in the middle, back through the glove, and by the time it entered his left hand, had spread slightly. It had crashed through his gloved left hand at an angle, ripping apart skin, bone, and cartilage before passing through the stout wooden case. It had flattened considerably while smashing the violin's neck and fingerboard before going through the bottom of the case and literally bouncing off Dieter's sternum, finally lodging between skin and clothing. Apparently, the second bullet had entered the case straight on, splintered the top and bottom of the instrument to irreparable pieces before exiting somewhere down and to the right after the first shot had knocked him backwards. All in all, it was astonishing. The two cops were right. The violin had certainly saved Dieter Bach's life.

Taliaferro pulled a chair close to the bed and took a deep breath. It had been a very long night and this wasn't going to be easy, but that was par for the course in his job. "Mr. Bach, I am very sorry about your violin. I really am, but we need to talk to you about your hands. Violins, even rare ones, can be replaced. Hands can't. We've got some pretty good surgeons here at Mercy, of course, and your hands are going to need a lot of surgery. Right away. Still, knowing your, ah, your occupation, I'd like to privately recommend you have it done at the Mayo Clinic. I did my training there, and I personally believe their men are the very best. Think about it. By the way, your manager is waiting to see you. You feel like talking to him a couple minutes?"

Dieter shook his head. "Sy? No, not just yet. Maybe later. I'm very tired. Thank you for everything you did."

"It's all right. Sleep's probably best. You need all the rest you can get these next few days. I'll check on you again in a little while."

Dieter heard the door close softly, but didn't see the young doctor leave. He *was* tired, but not in the least sleepy. He simply couldn't bear to open his eyes and look at his wrapped hands again. Nor did he wish to ever again have to glimpse that small coffin which held the broken body of his beloved Guad. He didn't want to see anything. Or anyone. Not for a long time. . .

Surgical expertise was primary, but that was not the only reason Dieter went to Mayo's. After he was released from Mercy (they needed the bed) he couldn't bear to go back to the Mayflower, and had nowhere else in the city to live. Sy offered his town house in Brooklyn Heights, but Dieter politely turned his generous manager down, knowing the house would be in shambles since Sy had divorced his third wife. Staying there for any length of time would have made his depression even worse. No, he'd had to get out of New York, away from the steady stream of friends, mostly other musicians, who had come to the hospital with flowers, and *sotto voce* words of condolence, which he knew were outwardly truthful, but he also knew that deep down inside, each one was secretly thanking God it was not him or her who might never play again. . .

"Might" is what the New York doctors had said, but after the second surgery on his left hand at the Mayo Clinic, Dr. Ralph Ennis knew it was hopeless, and so did Dieter.

"I'm sorry, but there is simply too much damage, Mr. Bach," Dr. Ennis said. "We can use some artificial parts and stainless steel pins, but there is no way we can repair the nerves. They have been virtually destroyed. After one, maybe two more operations, we may be able to fix it so you will have a little movement, but all your fingers will curl slightly at the same time. There will be no digital independence. You will never be able to make a fist, nor will you have much strength in this hand. It's doubtful you'll be able to carry anything such as a suitcase with it."

Mayo doctors tell it like it is.

Ennis pinched the bridge of his nose. Blew out his cheeks, and Dieter could tell the surgeon was trying very hard to form his next words carefully, but couldn't. "As for ever playing again, I'm very sorry, but no. It will be impossible. Believe me, I know how devastating this is to you. I'm a surgeon. If I had a similar accident, I don't know what I'd do with myself. But we have some good people here who can help you with that part of all this."

Dieter swallowed hard. "What about my right hand?"

"That's the good news. The bullet passed through clean. Minimal tissue damage. A little therapy, it'll be practically good as new. You should have full use of it within a few weeks. A month or two tops. Look, I've taken the liberty of setting up an initial session with Dr. Paul Kanakas. He's one of our very best, and also loves music.

Plays cello in our doctor's quartet."

"Mayo's has a string quartet?"

Ennis laughed. "Not officially, just a bunch of amateurs who get together once a week. They don't give performances, but there's usually a pretty good crowd at the host's house every time they tune up. I'm sure Paul will be a great help, especially now."

But Dr. Paul Kanakas was not a great help. Though he tried his best, he was no help at all. Neither were the two therapists Dieter spent hundreds of dollars on back in New York. The depression was far too deep. His life, which had been his career, was over. He had died inside. Had no direction. No ambition at all. No prospects. Couldn't bring himself to go to a concert, or a play, movie, or even to the library. Wouldn't read a newspaper for fear of seeing yet another article about his 'accident.'

To the man's everlasting credit, Kurt Mueller, an owlish German who had been a fellow student at Juilliard (and was now the third bassoon player in the Met orchestra) allowed Dieter to stay temporarily at his rent-controlled apartment at the Ansonia. Mueller didn't attempt to add more to his old friend's out-patient treatment either. Poor fellow, he was so neurotic it was all he could do to keep his own head above the water of sanity.

In the end, it was Sy Glazer who saved Dieter's sanity, and probably his life. One morning in late March, Sy called and asked Dieter to drive up to Westchester County with him to see his father. Dieter, so mired in the abyss of self-pity (or perhaps not paying much attention when Sy called) agreed to go along, not remembering Sy's father was in a nursing home. Sy didn't talk to him during the drive, sensing Dieter would not be very good chat-company anyway, and Dieter didn't really wake up until Sy led him through the foul-smelling halls to his father's room. The old man was asleep, so Sy took him back down one corridor after the other, pointing at the wretched inhabitants, some single and double amputees, who were trying their best to walk or pull their wheelchairs in one direction or another, and for some of them, it was with monumental effort. Sy said not a word, and the determination on the faces of those poor creatures was like a hard slap to Dieter's. Their world, their universe, was reduced to thirty meters of plaster walls and waxed linoleum floors. Even so, most of them were hobbling, shuffling, steadily pushing themselves along toward their goal— a day room with shelves full of *Reader's Digest* condensed books and a blaring television set. Though pathetic to watch, they were nonetheless *moving*. They had *not given up*.

Dieter muttered something of an excuse and ran out, his eyes full of tears of both humiliation and shame. He waited in the car for the hour Sy spent with his father. All the way back to the city, Sy was silent, allowing Dieter to run the full gauntlet of his feelings, which ranged from self pity to guilt to anger. He dropped Dieter off at the Ansonia Station, leaned over, and said, "Be at my office tomorrow morning at nine sharp. We have to map out a game plan for your new career."

"New career?"

"Yes, new career. You were one of the world's best violinists. No reason on earth you can't also be a fine conductor. See you tomorrow."

"Conductor?"

"You heard me. Nine sharp, Dieter."

◆

Chapter 2

Returning her smile, the policeman declined a second glass of mineral water offered by the charming Lufthansa flight attendant. He handed her his empty glass. "How long before we land, Fraulein?"

The efficient stewardess in First Class did not have to glance at her watch. "We will be making our final approach in thirty minutes, sir. Right on time."

The policeman nodded. He liked for things to be on time, whether trains, planes, whores— or informants. So far, his man in Buenos Aires had never failed to show up at the exact time and place for their five previously arranged meetings. He smiled again, this time at the top of the bald head of the snoring businessman sitting in front of him. Considerable amounts of hard cash, in crisp American dollars, were usually a dependable prod to punctuality. *Carrots always work better than sticks*. He shot his immaculate cuffs and reset his watch to the Buenos Aires time zone.

Eduardo Carrera paced anxiously in the dingy room on the fourth floor of the Hotel Europa that smelled of cheap wine, stale smoke, and recent sex. Carrera would have also liked a little drink, and maybe a cigar, either of which might settle his nerves. This was, of course, impossible because he knew the German policeman, who never smoked nor drank, would doubtlessly smell it on his breath, and be furious. Or at the very least, upset. And Eduardo Carrera knew he could not afford to make the policeman upset. Ever.

However, this time the information he had to sell was rock solid. In the past, his stuff had been sometimes spotty, sometimes very accurate, and occasionally good, except relayed just a little too late for the policeman to act upon it. In every case, though, the policeman had never shown an iota of disappointment. Never showed a loss of temper, but on the other hand, he had never once showed any gratitude either— except for the fat envelope. For a German, Carrera thought, he possessed seemingly unlimited patience. Better still, he had always paid Carrera handsomely for his efforts, no matter if the results of those efforts had been poor, mediocre, or excellent.

Carrera frowned, remembering the first time he had met the soft-spoken policeman from Germany, whose reputation had preceded him to South America. Known as *Der Jaeger*, the quiet man (who looked and dressed like any ordinary businessman) was West Germany's top Nazi hunter, responsible for successfully tracking down several of the rats that had abandoned the ship of Adolf Hitler's Third Reich shortly before its inglorious end. Some said he had been helpful to the Israeli commando group that kidnapped Eichmann back in 1960 even though he had been extremely young to be a top investigator. In Intelligence circles, many whispered that *Der Jaeger* was also an executioner. A West German special agent with a license to kill.

Carrera grunted. While such rumors had never been proven, he could readily believe them. The policeman was as cold blooded as they come. He had fished Carrera out of a seedy gay bar a few months after his dismissal from his own secret service job; a job which had slowly driven him to serious drink. His periodic booze binges had finally cost him dearly, especially since he had been unable any longer to keep his homosexuality in the closet. Still, he had, over the years, kept his many contacts alive, and when he was sober, Carrera was as good an undercover cop as ever— which was exactly what *Der Jaeger* had wanted, and had paid well for.

Carrera lit a cigarette, inhaling deeply. Well, at least this time they would not have to travel the length and breadth of Argentina, not to mention bribed forays into neighboring countries, which was always risky business. The man's thoroughness and tradecraft were unbelievable. His Spanish was almost as good as his English, and from the looks of his build, which his clothes belied, he would most likely be a deadly adversary if things ever got rough. Yet, there were limits to everything, and Eduardo Carrera knew that luck had something to do with it. Sooner or later, he might possibly run out—

Two soft raps on the door, precisely at six o'clock told Carrera the man had arrived. Nevertheless, he walked to the door and spoke through the crack, "Who is it?"

"Mr. Smith."

Carrera opened the door, let the man in, and closed it quickly. "You are the most punctual human being I have ever met."

The policeman didn't respond to the compliment. Instead, he put a gloved finger to his lips, reached into his coat pocket, took out a pad and pencil, and wrote"

NO TALK. WHERE IS HE?

Carrera grinned. The man was also the most careful person he'd ever met. After all, the room *could* be bugged. He took the pad and pencil and wrote:

PAN AMERICAN HILTON

SUITE 200

BOOKED THERE UNTIL TOMORROW

Again the pad changed hands.

GET YOUR COAT AND HAT. WE WILL WALK.

Outside, on the street, talk was possible, but Carrera knew he would not even smell his envelope until the German policeman had every scrap of information he wanted.

"Is he alone?"

"Yes. Last night he had a whore. High priced. Came in a limo, and stayed about an hour. Today, he had two visitors, one at two in the afternoon, one at four. Both as well dressed as yourself. Tonight he will probably have dinner at the restaurant there. I think it must be one of his favorites. He has dined there every night for a week."

"What time?"

"Promptly at eight. He's a big eater."

Without breaking stride, the policeman handed Carrera a plain white envelope that was instantly stuffed into a trouser pocket. "You have done well this time. If all goes as I wish, I will bring you a bonus next time."

Carrera asked, "Will there be a next time?"

"I am sure of it. Now, just to remind you, I know that in the past, you have been known to peddle certain information to the Americans and the British from time to time, and that is quite all right, so long as you always give me what I want. On the other hand, as I told you in the beginning, if I ever find out that you have shared any of *my* information with them, the Israelis, or anyone else, I will come back, find you, and kill you. You and your miserable boyfriend, too. And, I also promise it will not be a quick death. You do believe me, don't you?"

Carrera licked his lips and shuddered. "Yes, I believe you. I believed you the first time."

"Good. When you're sober, you are a wise man. Turn right at the next corner and go on about your business. I will be in touch."

Eduardo Carrera followed his instructions, and the policeman walked leisurely for another half hour before hailing a taxi. "The Pan American Hotel, please."

At seven, the policeman entered the hotel, headed straight for the restaurant, and ordered a bottle of mineral water at the bar. From the seat he chose, he could see every table reflected in the mirror. He nursed his drink for twenty minutes, then got up and walked to the headwaiter's desk.

"May I be of assistance, sir?" the man asked, affecting a slight, theatrical bow.

"Yes, please. I would like a table for dinner at eight."

"Are you a guest here, sir?"

"No, nor do I have a reservation, but your restaurant has been very highly recommended, and I would appreciate whatever you can do." With those words, he held up a folded bill. Its denomination caused the *Maitre d'* to lift one eyebrow in a high arch, and a double row of white teeth appeared below his pencil-thin mustache. Manicured fingers deftly took the American bill and deposited it into the inside pocket of his tuxedo jacket. "To be sure, sir. A fine table it will be, sir. Will you be dining alone?"

"Yes. I'll wait at the bar."

"Very good, sir. I shall call for you at eight sharp."

"Thank you."

The policeman returned to his seat at the end of the bar, ordered another bottle of mineral water and waited, ignoring the cigar and cigarette smoke being produced by the more serious drinkers. At five till, he spotted his quarry heading for a table in the far corner. The stout man was instantly recognizable. The policeman made a mental note to compliment his staff artist. His technique of doctoring – from a thirty year-old photograph – how a man's face had likely morphed was highly accurate. Both he and Carrera had indeed done well this time around. It was him, all right. No doubt about it.

Half an hour later, he found himself enjoying the sea bass and oyster meal, which he took his time over. He could have had two complete dinners in the time it took the fat man to consume his own, along with a whole bottle of red wine. While he was eating, the policeman studied his man, softly chuckling because the pig looked remarkably like the well-known German actor, Gert Frobe, in a scene from one of the James Bond films; the florid face, thinning hair, gold rings on chubby fingers, a diamond stickpin in his silk tie, a beautifully tailored suit that almost disguised his girth, and the dainty table manners of a diplomat.

The policeman dawdled over his dessert until the fat man ordered a second cup of coffee, and then signaled the waiter, handing him enough money to pay his bill plus a more than generous tip. He dropped his napkin on the table, stood, and walked directly over to the fat man's table and sat down across from him. *"Guten Abend, Herr von Bittnerhof."*

The startled man jerked upright in total surprise, but recovered just as fast, answering in perfect Spanish, "I think you have made a mistake, whoever the hell you are. My name is not von Bittnerhof."

The policeman cocked his head. "Yes, I am aware that here in Argentina you now go by the name of Wilhelm Tauber, and that you have used a dozen other aliases since you left Germany in 1945, but I know exactly who you really are, and almost everything else about you. There are only a few missing pieces I wish to fill in."

Pig eyes narrowed to slits. The voice became a hoarse whisper. "Who are you?"

The policeman laughed softly. "A policeman who works for the West German Government. My name and rank are unimportant, but I do have a certain reputation—as a hunter. A hunter of men."

The fat face went from beet red to pale white. *"Mein Gott in Himmel!* You...You're the one they call *Der Jaeger?"*

"Yes, but do relax, Herr Tauber. I am not here to threaten you with extradition, assassination, or any other unpleasantness. That is, if you cooperate. I merely wish for the two of us to have a nice, private chat. Shall we go up to your suite?"

With shaking hands, Tauber opened the door of his suite. The opulence of the sitting room was enough to elicit a complimentary comment from the policeman. "Very nice. You certainly live well. Please sit down. I mean you no harm. Really."

He waited until the obese man collapsed onto the larger of the two sofas, and then pulled an armchair up close. "Business is good, I take it."

Tauber wheezed, "Business is always good. What do you want from me?"

"In a moment. First, indulge me with a bit of history. Your real name is Alois Manfred von Bittnerhof, late of Hamburg, ship and U-Boat builder, one of Germany's five richest industrialists during World War Two, friend of Krupp, Thiessen, Hitler, and incidentally, user of hundreds of Jewish and Russian slave laborers. You were last seen at a camouflaged U-Boat facility at Trondheim, Norway in late April or early May of 1945.

"Abandoning a wife and six children to whatever fate might befall them, you bought your way to Argentina, by way of the 'rat line' as we call it now. First through Germany and Switzerland, then through Italy and Portugal, and by tramp steamer here, using several forged passports. It took you less than a year, although I imagine some of your journey was rather difficult.

"Once here, having transferred a considerable fortune through Swiss banks, you have been able to live like a Prince, and now you are the front man for a large cooperative of ranchers, selling beef to countries all over the world."

"All right. Yes, I was a Nazi. I don't deny it, but I committed no war crimes."

"Well, that is perhaps moot. All of you say that. Still, as a matter of fact, it is true that most of the money you spent on your escape was your own. You are not on my "A" list as a fugitive Nazi war criminal.

"It is also somewhat ironic that had you stayed in Germany, you might not have ever been arrested and put on trial. Even if you had been, you probably would have been given a light sentence, which, like many others, may have been greatly reduced. Our latter day German courts have shown amazing leniency to people like you, sad to say. But as far as I am concerned, and in spite of your physique, to me you are what the Americans colloquially refer to as small fry."

Tauber's face showed instant relief, but only for a second. "Then why have you chased me down?"

"Because I am after much bigger fish. Actually, the biggest one of all. Martin Bormann."

"Bormann? He's dead."

This time the policeman's demeanor turned ugly. "You will irritate me to the point of fury if you play stupid parlor games with me, von Bittnerhof. You and I both know he is not dead. I believe you know something about where he might be hiding, and you *will* tell me.

"I know you were the brains behind that farcical "Fourth Reich" organization. *Odessa* was never meant to do anything but cover your escaping asses should Hitler or Himmler have found out about it. My guess is that's why you included Bormann in your well-developed plan.

Had anything gone wrong, Bormann might well have convinced Hitler that Odessa was genuine. In any case, you and many others were quite successful. For that, you have my professional compliments. Now, tell me about Bormann."

Von Bittnerhof squirmed visibly. His stomach was not doing its job. Wasn't digesting at all. But acute indigestion was not his main source of discomfort. It had been a long time since he felt this frightened. This man with the soft voice and cold eyes could make big trouble for him in spite of the political and financial protection he had enjoyed for years. Worse, if he didn't get what he wanted, *Der Jaeger* could quite possibly make him *dead!* There was no way to bluff him, and it was useless to lie.

Von Bittnerhof grasped at one last straw. "If I tell you what I know, I might be killed."

The policeman's gray eyes became even colder. Reptilian. His voice was like the cutting edge of a new razor. "If you don't, there will be no 'might' about it. I know every way there is to kill a man, von Bittnerhof, and I am an expert in all of them. Especially the slow ones. Now, since you have nothing to lose, start talking. I have all night, and I am a very good listener."

He casually reached into a coat pocket and pressed the switch of the tiny *Blaupunkt* tape recorder. Its receiver was cleverly concealed in one of the coat buttons, not two feet away from the fat man's mouth.

◆

Chapter 3

Dieter was both surprised and flattered that Sy insisted on driving him down to North Carolina rather than putting him on a plane, although he understood Sy's reasoning. They'd rarely had enough time together for long conversations, and now, of all times, they needed some. Sy claimed it was the first time he had taken a more than a single day off from work in over ten years, and Dieter believed him, but this trip would hardly be a vacation for either of them.

They were somewhere south of Richmond when Sy said, "Stop thanking me, Dieter, I just didn't want to see my biggest meal ticket go down the toilet, that's all."

Over the years, Dieter had become used to Sy's version of humor. He was a past master of well-meant sarcasm. Dieter laughed and replied, "What gave you the idea in the first place?"

"Wasn't too tough to figure. One; way back when Margo DeLoach first called me about you, she told me all about your unique memory gift. I remember it almost word for word; 'The boy has something special, Sy,' she said. 'You know how Toscanini and others had that photographic memory, and could memorize a page of music in a glance? Well, this young man has something similar. He can actually write down on paper anything he hears, whether it's music or anything else. He has total memory recall. Plus, he can reproduce it. Not only does he memorize -- and I'm talking about with no effort at all -- the solo part of every concerto in the repertoire, he knows every note in the orchestral score as well, from flute to double bass – simply because *he's heard it*.

'It's amazing. I've only known one other violinist who had that. Nathan Milstein, though Milstein used to irritate the hell out of orchestra players when he'd hear wrong notes in rehearsals, turn around, and play their parts correctly, whether they were clarinets, trumpets, or whatever. I tell you, this kid is something else! Once he hears something, anything, he can play it perfectly. Of all the students I've had here at Julliard, he shows the most promise for a high-flying career. Good looking as the devil and fairly oozes charisma. He and that Perlman boy are the best to come along in a long while. You'd better come over here and listen to him play, and maybe sign him up before the wolves grab him.' "

"I remember," Dieter said. "And your memory gift isn't far behind mine. I couldn't believe you had brought a contract with you that very day."

"My good luck. We both owe Madame Margo a big one. Anyway, my feeling was that if you could learn your sonatas, concertos, and chamber music like that, why not the rest of the orchestral rep? You had a few conducting classes at Julliard, didn't you?"

"Yes. We all did, but I never gave it any thought."

"Why would you have? So, when I thought about it some more, I put two and two together and said to myself, if this guy can memorize scores simply by listening to them, all it would take for him to be a good conductor is to pick up some technique, and get some practical experience. Conductors don't have to use their left hands except for expression and dynamic control anyway, and most of them use their left hands far too much, in my opinion. So, all that seemed left to do was find somebody who could show you the technical ropes, and show you where the trouble spots are in the scores. And there is nobody in the world better at that than Lert."

Dieter knew what Sy said was the truth. In all of music, the two most renowned teachers of conducting still alive were Hans Swarowski and Richard Lert, but Swarowski lived in Vienna. Lert, however, lived in California, and had agreed to work with him, primarily based on his reputation as a violinist—
and probably because he had heard of what had happened, and felt sympathetic.

"I can't believe Dr. Lert agreed to take me," Dieter said. "He's very old, isn't he?"

"Ancient, but his mind is still sharp as a tack, and he may be thinking you are one last challenge for him. But it won't be any cakewalk, Dieter. He told me he's gonna treat you just like any other rookie stick swinger who comes to him, and they flock to him in droves. Most don't last two weeks. I've heard he can be merciless sometimes."

Dieter didn't respond to that, though he'd heard the same thing. He personally knew of men who had been washed out of Lert's conductor's workshops with musical insults of the lowest kind heaped like dung on their heads. He decided to change the subject. “Tell me about the house, Sy.”

“You’ll see it soon enough. It belonged to my aunt Sophie. Her husband was my uncle Isaak, Dad’s only brother. Uncle Ike, as I called him, did well in the jewelry business and left Sophie well off when he died. She could have lived anywhere, but Florida was too hot for her, so she bought a house at Manteo, on Roanoke Island. She’d been a hairdresser before she married Ike, and opened up a beauty shop in the house just to have something to do, along with her rose garden, which was hot stuff. Wasn’t long before the locals started calling her ‘One-eyed Rosie’.”

“Why?”

“Would you believe? She had an eye put out by a hummingbird. A damn *hummingbird!*”

Dieter knew it was totally disrespectful, but couldn’t help laughing. Sy laughed along with him, and added, “She wore an eye patch for the twenty more years she lived there. Same color as your glove. Black.”

Self consciously, Dieter rubbed his right hand over his left. The glove had been Kurt’s idea. A good one, too, since it drew less attention to his hand than the ugly, scarred, and practically useless appendage it had become. Dieter couldn’t stand to look at it uncovered, and was sure no one else could either. Thanks to the therapy -- most of which consisted of squeezing a tennis ball two hours per day -- his right hand had become normal again. This was a blessing, because he was finally able to at least eat without help, shave, and dress himself, though not as quickly as before.

Sy continued. "I used to come down here part of every summer before I got married the first time. Sophie and Ike never had kids, and I was her only nephew. I hated it when she called me Seymour, but other than that, I loved her to pieces. She left the house to me in her will. I never had the guts to sell it, and it has cost me a small fortune to keep it up, pay the taxes, and find other hairdressers to run the shop she established. Anyway, when the last one left just last month, I got the idea it would be a terrific place for you to hole up while you do your score study for Lert. You only have till July, you know, and distraction-wise, Manteo is about as far removed from New York as you can get."

By the time they reached North Carolina's Outer Banks by crossing the choppy Currituck Sound, Dieter began to doubt what Sy had said. Mile after mile after mile seemed like one long resort and strip mall, which it was, especially through Kitty Hawk and Kill Devil Hills. Eventually, past the famous area of Nag's Head, they crossed the causeway bridge over the narrow strip of water known as Roanoke Sound and were in the village of Manteo. Sophie's house, Sy said, was just a few blocks down on this, the main street, which was also highway 264 and which also led to a bridge across yet another sound (the Croatan) west to the mainland. Dieter's first impression of the island was positive. Charming. They drove down the lovely, green-bordered avenue where nothing moved very fast, like the "Elm Street" of so many books and movies. Everyone they passed waved at them, though none could have had the slightest idea who they were. He saw the Beauty Shop sign before he saw Sophie's house, which was set back about twenty meters from the street.

The moment they pulled into the driveway and got out of Sy's Lincoln, Dieter was pleasantly assaulted by the fresh smell of the local verdure; azalea, mimosa, hydrangea, and the descendants of Sophie's roses. It suddenly hit him very hard, that he had traveled over most of the United States. Had played in every large -- and many smaller -- cities from Philadelphia and Boston to San Francisco and Los Angeles. From Detroit and Cleveland to New Orleans and Dallas, but had never really seen (make that *experienced*) any one of them. It was a price all performing artists pay. What do they know of those places but their airports, hotel rooms, concert halls and taxicabs? Not much, discounting the impressive homes or condos used occasionally for post-concert receptions. Also, from the time he was fifteen, he had lived in Manhattan, in various apartments— or parts of them. Now, he was going to have a house, an *entire house*, all for himself for a few months, and in an actual real-live neighborhood in an honest to God small southern town. Dieter was in a very good mood when they walked up the creaking wooden steps, crossed a porch that sloped up slightly to the warped screen door, and walked into 'One-eyed Rosie's' Beauty Shop. The front door wasn't even locked!

After unloading everything, including Dieter's ten-speed bicycle, they drove further down the street to a German restaurant with the unlikely name "The Weeping Radish"-- a tourist magnet that sported its own brewery and beer garden! This time, Dieter was almost as hungry as Sy.

They had hardly taken seats in one of the high-backed booths when the most beautiful girl Dieter had ever seen appeared, her curly, long black hair hanging down around both sides of her neck and over the blouse of her mock-Bavarian *Dirndl.* She marched over to their table with a wide smile, and in the sweetest of southern accents, announced, “Hi, y’all, I’m Susan, and I’ll be your server this evening. Would you like something from the bar?”

She was absolutely stunning. Almost as tall as Dieter, with eyes too dark to be called brown, she had a smoky-golden complexion that could have easily been Mediterranean. The silly low-cut costume she wore did absolutely nothing to hide her terrific figure. They gave her an order for some of the home-made beer. Sy grinned at Dieter, noticing the way he watched the girl walk away toward the bar. “Looks like you’re coming back to life after all. Careful, Dieter, I know it’s springtime, but you’re down here to work.”

Dieter felt they apparently did not make much of an impression on ‘Susan’ that night. Sy Glazer was a big eater, but not a big tipper, and Dieter felt more than a little embarrassed when they left.

Sy stayed with him one more day before heading back to New York. It rained hard all day, and Dieter later experienced for the first time since his mugging how pleasant it was to sleep an entire night through-- without any dreams.

After Sy left, the first thing Dieter did was take down the beauty shop sign which he stored in the shed behind the house where Sophie had kept all her gardening tools and an antique lawnmower. He wondered if his left hand would be strong enough to push it, and resolved to try it the moment the grass needed cutting. He wouldn't have long to wait, either. It was astonishing how fast and how thick the grass grew on Roanoke Island.

The following day, the sun was out again, and Dieter decided to explore some before starting in on his studies. He rode the ten-speed from the eastern shore to the western shore, plus down some of the side streets that ran basically south from the highway. It didn't take long to ride through the quaint business area located on the northern tip of the island, around the tiny harbor. He'd decided to save the Lost Colony area until last, perhaps on a separate day altogether. Sy had already given him a brief history lesson of Walter Raleigh's luckless colonists, and of the outdoor drama written about them by Paul Green, which was performed nightly during the summer season.

After lunch, he struck out again and pedaled all the way down the eastern side of the island to the fishing village of Wanchese. Sy had said the main villages on the island had been named for two Indian chiefs who had been very different types of individuals. That seemed to Dieter *apropos*, since the physical characteristics of the two communities, and as he would soon discover, their residents, were as different as night and day. Though only a few miles apart, they seemed a world removed from each other. At the end of the day, he was exhausted. And hungry.

He went back to the German restaurant for dinner and was terribly disappointed that Susan was not there. It was her night off, the waiter told him. Dieter ate a light meal, went back to the house, and reviewed the list of repertoire Dr. Lert had sent for him to prepare. It was a list that confused Dieter totally. None of the great orchestral works were on the list! No Beethoven. No Brahms, or Strauss, or even Mozart, except for the well-known chamber work, *Eine Kleine Nachtmusik*. The only symphony on the list was the little B Flat symphony of Franz Schubert. There were short works by Grieg and Dvorak, and one string orchestra suite by the English composer, Benjamin Britten, a piece which he didn't remember ever having heard. Why these symphonic trifles?

He was more than a little disappointed, practically insulted, but thought the old man must have had some good reason for choosing these seemingly insignificant pieces. Little did he know, as he would find out. All too soon.

◆

Chapter 4

The policeman was not unhappy to be on a night flight back to Germany. Practically everyone around him was sleeping. He was also glad to have a window seat, and in his left ear, the tiny earpiece, which looked so much like a sophisticated hearing aid, could not be seen by anyone, nor could the ultra thin wire connecting it to the recorder, which he switched on. Its clarity was amazing. He closed his eyes and listened carefully to von Bittnerhof's opening recitation:

"I spent four years setting up Odessa. It was not easy, and yes, it required a lot of money. More than you might imagine, but then, most of the people who wanted to use our pipelines to South America had money. I naturally took a percentage for project expenses. Bormann came to see me out of the blue one day, saying he wanted to buy in. He personally brought me a small fortune as a token of good faith, and promised more. He had gotten my name from the highest sources in the Vatican. Don't ask me how.

"As everyone knows, the Peron government here in Argentina was rather sympathetic to our, ah, cause, at that time, and was very generous and discreet with their protection. Naturally, the first problem was how to get

out of Germany undetected by the Gestapo. Then, several safe routes through other countries had to be established and maintained. There were plenty of people who hated the Hitler regime enough to help: Partisans, trustworthy priests, farmers, shopkeepers, and ordinary citizens from one end of Europe to the other. It was no simple task to organize them all into a secret and effective network, with several alternative routes. I take a great deal of pride in how successful it was.

"It was slow going, however. Once here in Buenos Aires, I was able to stay in contact with everyone along the way. In Bormann's case, for example, it took until 1948 before he managed to get here. I know for a fact that on one leg of his escape, he spent three days and nights hiding beneath a cartload of manure, breathing through a piece of hosepipe. And to digress a little, yes, you are correct. When he first approached me in Hamburg, I knew that if any of Himmler's gang got wind of what we were doing, Bormann might well have persuaded Hitler that our purpose was to lay the foundation for a Fourth Reich elsewhere, that would ultimately rise again. Who knows whether or not that might have worked, but if anyone could have done that, Bormann could."

At that point, the policeman had interrupted. "When was the last time you saw Bormann?"

"At Trondheim, with Otto Skorzeny. They were outfitting a secret U-Boat Kellerman had supervised building. They didn't think I knew about it, but I did. I was hardly surprised, either. After all, I knew about two other U-Boats that had delivered money here previously. I had

sent them myself. Anyway, Bormann obviously had his own agenda and I was not about to interfere."

"It didn't take a genius to determine that he was planning to ship a huge amount of gold over here before making his escape. In any case, I didn't loiter around that complex in Trondheim long enough to make sure, though. The time was right for me to make my own move south, which I did. Trouble is, I don't believe that particular U-Boat ever made it to Argentina."

Again the policeman had broken in. "Why do you say that?"

"Because if it had, I would have known about it from Peron's people. No, it was either sunk somewhere en route, or it went somewhere else. Meantime, Bormann went back to Berlin, didn't he? His actions inside the Hitler Bunker are well known. It's too bad Skorzeny is dead. He might have been able to tell you more."

Here, the policeman had worked hard to suppress his laughter. This fat former Nazi couldn't have known that he *had* talked to Skorzeny, several times before his death in Spain. However, he listened politely as von Bittnerhof continued his redundant narrative.

"Let me tell you, Otto Skorzeny was one prominent Nazi who came out of it all smelling like a rose. He turned himself in after the war, got himself a smart English lawyer, and beat the rap! Walked out of court free as a bird. You may know that Skorzeny also eventually turned up here in Argentina. He totally reorganized Peron's police force, and according to my quite reliable sources, became Eva Peron's lover for a while."

Again, budding impatience had caused the policeman to break into the man's monologue. "Yes, yes, but you're slipping off the main track, von Bittnerhof. All that is unimportant to me. Get back to Bormann. What else do you know?"

"Probably no more than you. Back then, I read six international newspapers every morning, not that they were of much help. From what I gathered from my contacts, Bormann left the Hitler bunker right after the Fuehrer and Eva Braun committed suicide. My sources were positive he was wounded and rendered practically deaf while following a tank that got hit. Still, he somehow managed to get to the zoo, where one of Hudal's people found him and hid him until he was well enough to travel. At last, he reached Italy where he spent some time at Bolzano, and then nearly two years hiding in a monastery.

"After he arrived here, via ship, he moved around constantly, in and out of Argentina. I saw him a few times. It appeared that his health had begun to deteriorate. Last time I saw him, he seemed to have aged forty years. Acted like a scared rabbit. Didn't seem at all like the Bormann we all knew. There is also one other thing I don't understand."

Der Jaeger was now all ears. "What would that be?"

"The West German government has officially declared Bormann to be dead. All kinds of witnesses have testified to it. Bodies, skulls, dental records and the like were dug up in Berlin. STERN, DER SPIEGEL and several other publications made a big to do over it. Actually, if he wanted to, Bormann could legally go back home now as a

free man—under an alias, naturally."

"So, what is so confusing to you?" the policeman had wanted to know.

"Well, the question is, why? If your government knew Bormann had escaped and come here, why tell the whole world he is dead?"

This time the policeman couldn't help chuckling. "Come, now, von Bittnerhof, I credit you with a good deal more intelligence than you are showing. Why, you ask? Think about it. If Bormann believed he had been declared dead, and not in any more danger of capture and prosecution, wouldn't he be less careful about his hiding places and contacts?"

"Ah, yes. I understand. Disinformation, and at the highest level. But I have one more question."

"What?"

"Surely you must know where Bormann is now. I mean, that historian-writer named Farago sniffed him out more than four years ago and wrote all about it."

"That is true, to a point. Farago did indeed locate Bormann. Our government has gone to considerable efforts to discredit him and his work. More, as you put it, disinformation."

"Then why harass me about it? If you want Bormann, why don't you go directly to that modest place in Paraguay where he is now?"

"I have already been there. More than once."

At this statement, von Bittnerhof's face had showed utter confusion. *"None of this makes any sense to me. I presume you are responsible for what happened to*

Cuckers, Guenther, and a few others I happen to know about."

The policeman had played innocently along. "What do you think happened to them?"

"They were murdered."

"They were sanctioned."

"Is that what you call it now? I repeat, if you are intent on finding and 'sanctioning' Martin Bormann, you already know where he is, and you certainly have the wherewithal to do whatever you want with him. Why bother me?"

"In the first place, as I told you before, I needed you to fill in a few missing pieces, which you have done. In the second place, what you don't know is that the man who made his way out of the Hitler bunker, rode a few kilometers in the bed of a shit wagon, and now lives like a rabbit in Paraguay, is not Martin Bormann. He is an actor, or rather, was an actor, who has impersonated the former *Reichsleiter* for so long, he now thinks he *is* Bormann.

"It is my belief that Bormann also boarded that U-Boat at Trondheim, and, I agree with you, I don't think his ultimate destination was South America at all. I learned from Skorzeny that the captain of that boat was Korvettenkapitan Horst von Hellenbach, a man too intelligent and experienced to have gotten his specially equipped boat sunk. I further believe both he and Bormann are alive and well. I just don't know where. Not yet."

"And so then, what about me?"

"What about you?"

"What are your intentions—now?"

"I will report to my government, as usual. My job is only to find rats like you. What the government decides to do about them is not my decision. We are finished here, Herr von Bittnerhof."

The policeman had then stood, removed a card from a different pocket, and handed it to the sweating man. "If you think of anything else pertinent to our conversation tonight, call the number I have circled. Collect, if you like. Auf wiedersehen, Herr, ah, Tauber. Have a nice life."

The policeman replayed the tape over and over until its batteries went dead. Only then did he allow himself to drift into a light sleep.

◆

Chapter 5

Dieter went back to the "Weeping Radish" for dinner every night. He was still self conscious eating in public, but had finally learned how to wedge his fork between the thumb and forefinger of his gloved hand firmly enough to hold a sausage or piece of meat down while he sliced it with the knife. He'd make all the cuts, then hide his deformed hand under the table or under his napkin while he ate. The reason Dieter went back there was not that he craved Bavarian food that much. In fact, he was sick of it. He simply wanted to somehow get to know Susan.

It took two weeks. Exactly fourteen days, or rather, fourteen consecutive nights before the only other thing she said to him (aside from taking his order) was, "Is everything okay?"

On the fifteenth night, she plopped herself down opposite him in the same booth he always took -- always in her work-station area—and said, "Are you ever going to ask me for a date?"

"I'm sorry?"

"You come in here every night for two weeks, like this was the only place on the island to eat. You'd have to be a real German to do that. Either that, or you're trying to make up your mind about asking me for a date. Which is it?"

Dieter was so taken aback, all he could think of to say was, "But I am a real German." *Idiot! Why didn't you go ahead and ask her?*

"You don't talk like one. You sound just like any other American to me. A Yankee, that's for sure, but American just the same." Her smile was as lovely as the rest of her.

"I've lived in the United States since I was fifteen, but I really am German. I was born in a town called Freiburg, in the Black Forest region. That's in south Germany, so technically speaking, I am also southern, just like you."

"Really. What's your name?"

Dieter realized he must have looked like a complete fool, still holding his fork suspended between plate and mouth. He felt himself actually blushing when he said, "It's Dieter. Dieter Bach."

"Finally! Well, hey there, Dieter Bach. How do you spell Bach?"

"B-a-c-h, not B-o-c-k."

"Mine's Susan Everette. Two "t's" and an "e" on the end."

"I'm very pleased to meet you, Susan. I have wanted to."

"Taking your time about it, weren't you? Well? What about it? Are you going to ask me for a date or not?"

By now Dieter had recovered somewhat. "If I asked, would you give me one?"

"You do talk kinda funny, now that I've heard you say something. Okay, sure, I'll 'give you one.' I thought with the way you've been eyeballing me, you'd have asked me two weeks ago."

"I didn't know if you might be... you know—"

"Married or something? Not hardly. Are you rich?"

She had caught Dieter again by surprise. He certainly was not expecting that kind of question, but his brain was now working a little better. "Why would you ask that?"

"Well, I've spotted you all over the island, riding a bike. People who do that around here are either poor and can't afford a car, or rich tourists who ride a bike 'cause it looks fashionable. From the look of the clothes you wear in here every night, I'd say you were rich. Did you buy One-eyed Rosie's house?"

Dieter laughed. "You know, you ask a lot of personal questions before you date somebody, don't you? But to be honest with you, no, I am not rich. I'm not a poor man, but I'm hardly what you would call rich, either, and I am renting the house."

"Uh-huh. So, you're telling me you don't have a car because you don't want one? Is it hard to eat like that with one hand? What's wrong with your other one? Why do you wear a glove on it all the time? That's why you don't drive a car, isn't it?"

Dieter was determined things were progressing far too well to get upset about that particular barrage. "I don't own a car, Susan. I never learned how to drive."

"You kidding me? Where have you been living all your life, on Pea Island or behind the moon?"

"New York. I live in New York City."

"People drive cars in New York City, don't they?"

"If they're smart they don't."

"Well, how're you gonna drive me home tonight without a car?"

By this time Dieter had finally figured out that she was teasing him unmercifully, but in a lighthearted way, and gave her his best smile. "I could walk you home."

"Too far."

"Manteo isn't that big."

"Roanoke Island is. I live in Wanchese. Tell you what, you stop by about eleven, and I'll walk *you* home. Deal?"

"It's a deal."

"Okay. You know, you're a damn good-looking guy for a German-Yankee tourist, Dieter Bach, and I love that ponytail. But if I ever take you home to meet my Mama and Daddy, you'll have to cut it off."

"Wait a minute," Dieter said, catching her by the elbow. "I'm only asking you for a date, not to marry me!"

She tossed her mane of ebony curls, touched a finger to his cheek, bent down and whispered, "I wouldn't be surprised if you did someday, Mr. Bashful Bach. Wouldn't be a bit surprised." With those words, and a wink, she turned and left, taking the check with her. Dieter left, slightly dazed, a little disgusted with his reticence, but completely captured by her charm.

And was back at eleven sharp. But Susan Everette-with-two-"t's"-and-an-"e"-at-the-end did not walk him home. She led Dieter to the rear parking lot, cranked the starter pedal of a medium-sized Japanese motorcycle, revved it a few times, and told him to climb on behind her. Dieter had never been on a motorcycle, didn't have any idea what he was supposed to hold on to, and told her so.

"Put your arms around my waist. If you can ride a bike, you can ride one of these. I won't go fast, I promise," she said.

Dieter started to ask her if they shouldn't be wearing helmets, but swallowed the words as she roared out of the parking lot. He held onto her small waist for dear life, thinking that if Sy Glazer could see him doing this, he'd have cardiac arrest. Susan laughed the entire short time it took to reach the house, the sound of it trailing behind them like jet stream, and Dieter's knees were shaking when he climbed off in the driveway, not sure it was because of the speed, exhilaration, or something else. She kicked the stand down, leaned the red beast over, and said, "You got a Pepsi or a Mountain Dew? I need one for the road."

Dieter had not stocked any soft drinks, but she was happy enough with the Heineken he brought her, and they sat on the tilted front porch in the twin rocking chairs, which had been left there for years, talking. Well, as it turned out, Dieter did most of the talking. She wanted to know everything. Briefly as he could, he told her how at the age of fifteen, he'd been sent to study at Julliard, had been very lucky, and had won a pair of important competitions which had propelled him into a very successful career as a concert violinist until his 'accident.' "I was the victim of a mugging outside my hotel in New York, Susan. Shot through both my hands. I had several operations, and the surgeons did the best they could, but the end result is that I can never play again. I thought my life and career were over."

"Jesus!"

"I was very depressed, until my manager came up with an idea for me to become a conductor. Later this summer, I'm going to a workshop and find out if I can. I will be studying with a master conducting teacher named Lert. My manager owns this house, and has more or less loaned it to me for the summer. As you may imagine, I have a lot of preparation to do. At this point, my future as a performing musician is a big question mark."

Susan sipped on the one beer the whole time, watching his face, but never once interrupted. When Dieter asked about her own life, she chuckled and told him there wasn't that much to tell. She'd had three years of business school classes at Dare Community College, worked off and on at the restaurant to pay for them, and had never been out of North Carolina.

"Were you born here?"

"No, not on this island. I'm a Banker," she replied. Dieter had no inkling what that meant, and waited, thinking an explanation might follow, but she had fallen silent, and offered none. He watched her, as surreptitiously as he could, knowing that he had never met anyone even remotely like her. Not in his whole life. It was not as if he hadn't had experiences with women. He had, but they had all been of the casual one-night stand variety with those who were so often 'available' after concerts here and there, and meant nothing more to him than the late night dinners that followed receptions had; like an earned dessert. A temporary release valve for the inevitable emotional build up he always got when playing. He couldn't even remember any of their names, nor which city he'd met them in. This girl was different. Fascinating. Refreshing, and brassy as a Rossini Overture.

At last she said, "Dieter, you're probably famous, and I'm ashamed to admit I've never heard of you. I don't know anything about classical music or symphony orchestras and all, but I'd like to. I mean that."

Dieter went inside and fished out of the stacks his own recording of the Tchaikowsky Violin Concerto, which he'd done with the Chicago Symphony just after winning the Tchaikowsky competition. He handed it to her. Squinting, she read the jacket, and gave him a look that melted him all the way down to his shoes. Then she did an extraordinary thing. She took his left hand, brought it to her lips, kissed it lightly, and said. "I think I understand what it means for you to never be able to play again. I hope to God this new thing works out for you."

With that, she got up, walked down the steps toward the motorcycle, turned suddenly, ran back up the steps and kissed him full on the lips. Her voice was softer. Contrite. "I'm sorry about kidding you tonight at the restaurant. About that marriage stuff, I mean. I'll go out with you, Dieter. Tomorrow, or any time you want to. Who knows, one of these nights, I might even go to bed with you, but no marriage talk, even teasing. Men like you don't marry women like me. Not down here or in New York or Europe either."

"Why not?" he managed, trying to make it sound hypothetical.

"Look at me, Dieter. I'm over thirty years old. Why do you think I'm not already married?"

"I don't–"

"Because I'm black. Up north, people might call me a light-skinned African American. I'm what a lot of people down here still call an uppity high-yeller nigger gal."

The roar of her departing motorcycle did not overpower the ringing in his ears.

◆

Chapter 6

The following morning, June first, was Dieter's birthday. Having no appetite for breakfast, he sat in his robe at the kitchen table drinking coffee after his shower, knowing it would be useless to attempt any kind of serious work, although his self-imposed schedule for the day was relatively light. (To finish reading Max Rudolf's lofty book on conducting technique.) He sat there an hour, thinking about what Susan Everette had said. The more he thought about it, the angrier he became, especially when he remembered the look of sadness and resignation on her face as she said it. That face had not been created for frowning. It was not a face meant to be unhappy. Suddenly, Dieter knew what he wanted to do on this, his birthday.

He dressed and rode to the small shopping center, which was nearby. Some days before, he had glimpsed a barber pole just around the corner from the grocery store, on Pine Street. He walked into Smitty's Barber Shop just after nine, and found the proprietor asleep and snoring in his own chair, with part of a newspaper on his lap. The rest had fallen to the floor. A small bell attached to the door awakened him, and he jumped up with a start. "Mornin', mornin.' Have a seat."

Dieter took his place in the chair and allowed himself to be draped. Smitty, now wide awake, flipped the still-damp ponytail outside the paper collar he wound around Dieter's neck, saying, "What'll it be?" He turned the chair so that Dieter could see himself in the mirror.

"A haircut, please." Dieter couldn't help but notice his own wry smile as he said those words— the first time he had in nearly twenty years.

"Yessir. One haircut comin' right up. Um, how much of this you want me to cut off?"

"All of it."

The thin, bald barber hesitated only a moment, then twisted the chair back around, as if his new customer couldn't bear to watch what was going to happen. Then he asked Dieter something that evoked genuine laughter. "You want to save these two rubber bands?"

"No, I won't have any more use for them."

Smitty—whatever his last name was—went right to work. Dieter couldn't see what was happening, though he knew with certainty that losing those foot-long blond locks would forever end the persona of Dieter Bach, the Golden Boy of the Violin— a term Sy's publicity agent had thought up years ago. It was a gimmick that Dieter had always been a little embarrassed by, although it had done his career no harm. Just the opposite, in fact. Gradually, Dieter realized the barber was talking to him. "From up north, are you?"

"Yes, from New York."

"Thought so. Down here for long?"

"Possibly all summer."

"Been to the Lost Colony yet?"

"No, not yet, but I do plan to."

"Thought you might have been one of those perfessional actors. You sure got the looks of one"

"No."

"I had a small part in it a few years. Played one of the colonists. Didn't have no speakin' part, mind you, but it was always a lot of fun. You're the fella lives in One-eyed Rosie's house, ain't you?"

Dieter started to nod, but didn't, sensing it might cause Smitty's busy scissors to slip. The barber's casual remark brought home to him that by now, probably every native in Manteo knew who was occupying the rose garden house. Dieter decided to turn the tables on him. "Do you by chance know the Everette family?"

"Sunday Everette's family? 'Course I do. Her, Charlie, and Suzi. Wanchese folks. Ain't nobody on the whole island who don't know 'em. Sunday's 'bout the most respected colored woman on the island *or* on the Banks. Somethin' of a local legend. Charlie, now, don't know too much about him 'cept he's a mighty good charter boat captain. And that Suzi, well, it's a shame."

"Sorry?"

"What I mean is, she's purty as a china doll, but down here, a mixed race gal like her's got two chances. Slim and none. Like I said, it's a damn shame, you ask me. That gal could pass for white anywhere, I reckon. I'm surprised she ain't never left the island to do just that."

Dieter didn't respond, and for a while the only sound in the shop was the snip-snip of sharp scissors. After a while, Smitty paused. "You want a square neck or regular?"

"Regular, I guess." He felt the not unpleasant hum

and vibration of the electric clippers on the back of his neck below the paper collar, a few more strokes of brush and comb, and was swiveled around so he could see the results.

"Hmm," Smitty said, "Looks like you just growed up!"

It was true. The Golden Boy was gone. Dieter was looking at the face of a thirty-something man, with a normal combed-and-parted haircut. Someone new. Almost a stranger. Smitty undraped him, and he stood for a moment amidst piles of his own hair. At that time, Dieter didn't know that seven-fifty was a ridiculously low price for a haircut, but had presence of mind enough to tell the man to keep the change from the ten-dollar bill he handed the grinning barber. Smitty thanked him profusely, asked him to stop in again anytime, and Dieter told him he would.

Smitty's parting remarks were strange, however, and rekindled Dieter's anger. "Suzi's always in the pageant. Every summer. Plays one of the Indian gals. Don't have to use a wig or much makeup on her neither. Y'all come on back soon, now, y'hear?"

Dieter decided he didn't like Smitty very much. It seemed that the skinny barber had told him a lot, but had he really? Except for learning Susan's nickname, and the inference that her father was a white man, Dieter had learned nothing.

It took him most of the day to find a store that had a full length mirror in stock. Looking at his image in the Barber shop mirror had reminded Dieter he needed a large one to watch his practicing the baton technique so meticulously diagrammed in Rudolf's book; beat patterns for the "French School", the "Italian School" and the "German School of Conducting"—all of which were different. He would need to memorize, by thousands of repetitions, each of them until they were like second nature, and he would never have to mentally be concerned where in the air his baton was when he moved his wrist and arm.

Dieter knew this would be tedious work, but thought no more of it than how he formerly practiced his scales. Thus, after laboring hard to get the heavy mirror hung in the living room, he set about working on the most basic ones: Two beats per measure, three, then four, then six, humming melodies from various pieces of repertoire as he went along.

Before he knew it, it was time for dinner again. He needed another shower, took one, and stared at himself in the bathroom mirror, not knowing how he should comb (brush?) his hair—what was left of it. Finally he decided not to comb it at all, and just let it fall down naturally, whichever way it would, but was pleased that now, it didn't take very long to dry!

Dieter dressed in jeans and a tee shirt for a change, and rode his ten-speed to the "Weeping Radish". Without the slightest compunction, he walked straight to Susan's work station, and stopped her practically in mid-stride. She was carrying a full tray of food. "Susan," he announced, "I want you to look at my new haircut. If I ever do ask you to marry me, my hair should not be a source of objection to your parents. Also, I want you to know that I don't care if you are black, white, red, or any other color. I am not a prejudiced man, neither are my actions controlled or influenced by any other people. I make my own decisions, and today's decision is that I want you to stop by on your way home tonight so that we can discuss all this properly."

With that high-minded speech, he turned and stalked stiffly out of the restaurant, not waiting for an answer or caring one whit how many people--wait staff or customers--had heard him. Several must have, since the only sounds echoing in his ears were those of his own footsteps.

Shortly after eleven, he went out on the porch, knowing she would at least have to pass the house even if she didn't stop. No more than five minutes more went by before he heard the approaching roar of the Kawasaki. She pulled to the curb and said, "Climb on, I want to show you something before we have that talk."

They exchanged no words on the moonless ride through the dark pine and cypress to Wanchese. Susan negotiated a rough path at the end of a dirt road by the docks to a small, weather-beaten house trailer that sat no more than fifty yards from the water's edge. The tide was out, and the smell of rotting fish and seaweed wafted over them, borne on the gentle southwesterly. Susan shut down the motorcycle's engine and pointed to the trailer. "That's where I live. Impressive, isn't it?"

Dieter didn't know what she expected him to say in response, or how she felt he would react, so he said nothing in reply.

"The rent I pay for it isn't much, and it'll do unless a hurricane blows through and plants it in the sound. Come on in."

The door was not locked. Dieter had the fleeting thought that the natives of Roanoke Island were surely a trusting lot. Susan walked in ahead of him and began turning on lights. Dieter had never been inside one of these mobile homes, and was slightly surprised that he found himself standing in a complete house— only in miniature. There was a living room, a kitchen, a bedroom, and a bathroom, all perhaps less than half the size of normal proportions. And, everything was neat and clean as a hospital. The furnishings looked old, but comfortable, and there were flowers everywhere; hanging from the ceiling, in window boxes, and in tiny pots scattered all around. "It's nice, Susan, but I was under the impression you lived with your parents."

"Not since I graduated from high school." Susan chuckled, crossed her arms in front of her, continuing, "Now I have more room than they do."

She saw the look of confusion on his face, took his hand and led him back outside. Without another word of explanation, she started the motorcycle again, gesturing for Dieter to climb on. They rode to the docks and she pointed to a large trawler berthed nearest the channel. "That's Mama's boat. She and Daddy live aboard."

"They live on a fishing boat?"

"Yep. Happy as clams, and with just about the same amount of space."

The boat was as dark as the night around it. The fact that Susan had said, 'Mama's boat' instead of 'Daddy's boat' or 'Mama and Daddy's boat' struck Dieter as a little strange, but he decided not to pry. "They must be asleep."

Susan laughed softly. "Oh, sure. They'll be casting off before sun up. Come on, I want to show you something else."

By now Dieter was not surprised at the amount of traffic heading towards Nags Head, even well after midnight, and assumed that was Susan's destination. It wasn't. After crossing the high bridge, she turned right on the beach road and after a mile or two, Dieter quickly surmised they were the only two human beings on it, and going very fast.

Susan turned her head and yelled something back to him, but all he managed to salvage was "Bodie Island." The road was like a black ribbon laid between the pale breasts of sand dunes, and Dieter realized it paralleled the shoreline, with gentle curves every so often, but mainly a straight line. They passed, either way, not one single vehicle, and the telephone poles flew by like measure bars, much too fast to count them. Dieter saw no cottage, house, or anything else of human existence. It was as if the southernmost part of Nags Head had been the very end of the world. The dead end of the avenue of life.

After another mile or so, Susan took her right hand off the handlebars, pointing ninety degrees to the west. In the distance, Dieter made out the blunt shape of an unlit lighthouse, and once more plucked the word "Bodie" from Susan's vocal slipstream. What seemed like only seconds later, they came to a long, curved bridge, which in the darkness looked like some modern day dragon, or giant Anaconda, stretching across a wide inlet. Susan slowed down enough to tell Dieter they were now crossing the Oregon Inlet, and were now on Pea Island.

Before he could no more than register in his mind that Pea Island looked even more desolate than Bodie Island had, Susan yelled back, "Hold on tight!" and abruptly left the paved road. She plowed through sea grass and over high dunes right down to the Atlantic before turning sharply to the right. They raced down the wet sand for another few miles before she slowed, looked to her right, and stopped.

Dieter's legs were rubbery as he climbed off the Kawasaki. "Susan, how fast were we going?"

She didn't answer. Instead, she grabbed his hand and led him up the slope of sand perhaps a hundred yards to a pile of scattered, rotten boards. Edges of some of them were still buried in the sand, among pieces of broken bricks and mortar. "Remember the kids' story of the big bad wolf and the three pigs?" she said, laughing. " ' I'll huff and I'll puff and I'll blo—ow your house down!' "

Dieter stared at the rubble, grinned indulgently at her and asked, "Is this what you risked both our lives to see?"

Her face grew serious. The smile disappeared. "You need to see where I came from, Dieter. I wish you could have seen this shack before the storms blew it down. Two tiny rooms and a smokestack chimney. It was a thousand times uglier than my trailer is. This is where my parents first lived. Like I told you, I'm a 'banker', but as far as I know, I'm the only one who was ever conceived here on Pea Island."

Dieter took her in his arms then, and held her close. What little breeze there was blowing was blocked by the high dunes above them, and they stood like that for several minutes, listening to nothing but their own breathing and heartbeats. Gradually, Dieter felt himself becoming aroused. Susan apparently noticed it as well. She broke away from him and ran past the motorcycle to the ocean. Dieter watched in amazement as she yanked her shorts down and began unbuttoning her blouse. "Let's go swimming!"

Dieter took a few unconscious steps toward her, but hadn't closed the gap by half when she flung her blouse to the ground, and in the next instant dropped her bra and panties as well. She stood facing him for only a moment before turning and running into the surf, her hair flying. Dieter, of course, had stopped dead in his tracks at the first sight of her nakedness; her beauty having also struck him utterly speechless.

He didn't remain a mute statue for long, however. The next minute, he stripped and ran splashing to her, but she slithered out of his arms, like an eel. Dieter was oblivious to whether the water was warm or cold. It must have been warm, though, because it did not produce the same effect on him a cold shower would have, nor did he care. He looked around, then down. He thought he saw a shape gliding through the shallow water, but it vanished quickly. He started to wish aloud for moonlight, but was caught short of it by the feel of her body against his back, her arms around him. This time, turning, Dieter seized her arms and did not let go. The Atlantic stood still for the length of their first kiss, and he only released her when he felt the steady pressure of the resuming current against his legs, rocking him backwards with surprising force.

Susan clung to him. Grasped his face in her hands. "It's the undertow, Dieter." She had felt it as well. "We have to be careful not to go out too far."

Dieter had no recollection of how long they stayed in the deceiving, mild surf, splashing and ducking each other like children, nor did he have an accurate time frame of the memory of making love at the base of the dunes. He would never remember how many times they did. There were no words in either his German or his English vocabularies to vocalize what he was feeling, nor enough to ever describe the symmetry of their lovemaking. Still, the full understanding, the total understanding of the two words, "Love" in English and "Liebe" in German both blistered his tongue and ears at the same time he said them and heard them said back, knowing they were the first truth. The second truth, which came to him shortly after, before sleep kidnapped them, was that he knew with complete clarity that he never wanted to face another day without this woman at his side. The third truth was also a welcome surprise. Mother Nature had most certainly agreed with him, for she sealed dreams and those waking thoughts upon his eyes with the imprint of the most magnificent sunrise the world had ever seen.

Their forms, a single impression of shadow, must yet be engraved like lovers' initials into the sand of that dune on Pea Island.

◆

Chapter 7

The veteran trainer at the crowded police gym threw a towel at the rookie, who was overextending himself. "Take it easy, son. Rome wasn't built in a day, and neither is a great physique. You have to learn more about pacing yourself. If you don't, you could do your body more harm than good."

Out of breath, the young cop wiped his dripping face and grinned at his instructor. "Right. I know. It's just that..."

"What?"

The rookie inclined his head in the direction of a man working the circle of strength machines. "Look at that guy. I'm much taller, much younger, weigh a lot more than he does, and yet he handles almost twice what I can."

The trainer nodded. "True, but he's been at it a lot longer. When he's in town, he comes in three times a week, always at exactly the same time, and always does the exact same routine. Religiously. I could set my watch by him. He does a hard two-hour workout with the weights and machines, then a fifteen-minute sauna, and finishes up with a two-kilometer swim."

"He's in fantastic shape", the rookie said. "Big as I am, I'd hate to tangle with him. Who is he, anyway?"

"You don't know?"

"No. Never saw him outside the gym. He somebody important?"

The trainer's face turned thoughtful. "Well, let me put it to you this way. That man is the youngest one ever to graduate from the Academy. He's brilliant as he is tough. People who work with him say his mind works even harder than his body does. I can't believe you've been on the force six months now and don't know who he is."

"Come on, Max. Tell me."

"Have you ever heard of *Der Jaeger?"*

The rookie's mouth dropped open. "My God! That's *him?"*

"That's him."

"Damn! The man himself. I'd like to meet him."

Max the trainer laughed. "Not today, kid. Maybe in a year or two. Besides, I'm sure he already knows who you are."

"Really?" Surprise was added to the rookie's awe.

"He probably knows your girlfriend's name, your academic record, your pistol scores, the lot."

"So you think I'd best not walk over and introduce myself, sort of casual like?"

"I wouldn't if I were you. Only thing that man lacks is a sense of humor. All right, enough jabbering. You're cooling off. Give me ten more reps on that machine..."

After his swim, the policeman showered, dressed, and glanced at his watch, softly grunting with satisfaction.

Eight o'clock. On time. He left the gym through the back door to where he had left his car parked. The three year-old black Mercedes was as nondescript as any in Germany, but was always kept in top running condition. He drove down by the river to a small, discreet restaurant where he took most of his meals and within a few minutes was silently and slowly enjoying a tender *Roulladen* dinner, with a glass of simple Mosel. Two cups of strong coffee accompanied his desert—fresh fruit and good Danish cheese.

Fifteen minutes after paying his bill, he let himself into his apartment, which was in a building not four blocks from his office. He checked his phone messages. There were none, so he walked over to his stereo and put on a stack of his favorite recordings, beginning with the music from Grieg's *Peer Gynt*. Next, he poured himself a neat brandy and settled into his favorite armchair to wait for Hilde. Knowing she would come at exactly ten, he had left his door unlocked. He removed his weapon and placed it inside the drawer of the side table next to his chair, and loosened his tie. He took one more sip of the Cognac and smiled just as Hilde came through the door. On time.

"How are you? You look quite lovely, as always," he said.

Hilde Becker closed the door behind her and turned the key. "Thank you. I am well. And you?"

"I'm fine. I had a good day. Would you like a drink?"

"I'll have whatever you're having."

"Help yourself. You know where everything is."

Hilde's manufactured smile showed beautiful, even teeth. She certainly did know where everything was. There wasn't all that much in his apartment anyway. After coming here twice a month for the past five years, she knew the place as well as she did her own: Sparsely furnished living room, seldom used kitchen, bedroom and bath, all spotless. Hilde had often wondered if he had a cleaning woman, but had never asked. He didn't like for her to ask questions. She dropped her coat on the sofa, walked to the tiny bar and poured herself a couple sips. Turning towards him, she raised her glass. *"Prosit."*

"Gleichfalls. Is the music to your liking?"

"It's fine." She sauntered over to his chair and handed him the weekly slip of paper from the health department, which he glanced at briefly and dropped on the coffee table.

Hilde put her drink down and began her routine. He liked the never changing ritual, which was no more than a slow strip show. She always made sure to wear his favorite underwear every time, varying only their colors. One by one, shoes, dress, slip, garters and stockings, and finally her bra and panties came off in slow motion and were dropped carelessly on the carpet, until she finally stood before him naked. This she did with no little pride. She knew she still had a magnificent body; one that attracted and held a short but impressive list of clients, mostly highly placed older men in the Bonn government.

Without taking her eyes from his, she moved slowly into the second stage. She knelt before him and began undressing him, starting with his shoes and socks. He made only minimal movement to help her. When that was done, she stood, turned her back on him and walked like a runway model into the bedroom.

Not another word passed between them after he also came in, sat down on the edge of the bed and waited for her to slip a condom over his erection, and then stretch out on her back. He entered her immediately, and she began stage three; writhing and moaning as if it was the most stimulating sex she had ever had. In less than a minute, it was over. She lay beneath him a while longer, still whimpering and twitching as though she was descending from an Alpine peak of pleasure.

When he eventually rolled off her, she gently removed the condom from his limp organ, carried it to the bathroom, dropped it into the waste bin, and brought a warm washcloth back into the bedroom. While washing him, she murmured, "You are one strange man. You know I stay clean, yet you always insist on using those disgusting rubbers. You have a terrific body, too, and you're not a bad lover. I don't know why you don't find yourself a cute little *hausfrau* somewhere and settle down. Your love life would certainly be cheaper."

He chuckled. "We've had this conversation before, haven't we? I don't need or want that kind of responsibility. If you're tired of coming here, I can always find someone else. Bonn is full of attractive whores."

Hilde sighed. "I wish you wouldn't call me a whore."

"Right. You're just a modern businesswoman, and we have a deal; you sell, I buy."

"Will you call me for a week from next Friday?"

"If I'm in town."

"Well, then, *wiedersehen.*"

He didn't answer, so Hilde got up, dressed, reached for the envelope on top of the mantel and deposited it in her purse. She knew she didn't have to count it. Four hundred marks richer, she unlocked the door and left. She had plenty of time to visit another client; one whose name she actually knew.

The policeman stood and walked naked back into his living room. He locked his front door, then went to the bathroom and showered. He dried off, put on his robe and went back to his chair. He had a few sips of the brandy, watching the clock on the mantel. As the eleventh hour chimed, his phone rang. *Right on time.* "Yes?"

"Happy birthday, son."

"Thank you, *Mutti.*"

"Did you have a good day?"

"Not bad."

"Good. Did you get the present I sent?"

"Yes. The attaché case is very nice. Elegant. I will get a lot of use from it."

"Are you making any progress since your last trip to South America?"

"A little. You remember what one of your old American boyfriends used to say, don't you?"

"Which one? What saying?"

" 'By the yard, it's pretty damn hard. By the inch it's a cinch.' "

"Oh. Well, you'll get it done. I know you will."

"Thanks for your call, *Mutti*, I've got to get some sleep now."

"All right. Stay in touch."

"Always. Goodnight."

He had been in bed for only half an hour when his phone rang yet again. Angrily, he yanked it from the bedside table. "Yes?"

"This is, ah, Wilhelm Tauber. You said I should call if I remembered anything. I realize I may be calling late, but—"

The policeman was instantly alert. "Never mind that, Tauber. What is it?"

"I suddenly remembered something about my initial conversation with Bormann at Hamburg, some of which was rather humorous. We were kidding around, and he said he eventually planned to settle in America. As I recall, I told him if that was what he wanted to do, he should skip South America altogether, take his money and sneak ashore somewhere on the southeastern United States coast, which was lightly populated and where security was practically nil. He scoffed at the idea, and I forgot all about it.

"This morning, I got to thinking about it all again. If what you said is true, and that actor fellow in Paraguay we all thought was Bormann is really an imposter, it may be possible that Bormann actually *did* follow my whimsical suggestion. I mean, why were Bormann and Skorzeny up there at Trondheim in the first place? At that time, I thought Hitler had sent them up there for some crazy reason, but now I'm not so sure. What I'm telling you now may be nothing more than coincidence, but I thought I had better call you anyway."

"I'm glad you did. I don't believe in coincidences. I know that Bormann boarded that U-Boat, along with more than fifty millions of Hitler's gold he had stolen. Skorzeny told me that much, but like you and everyone else, Skorzeny had assumed the boat would be heading to South America. Thank you for the call, Herr von Bit—Herr Tauber, and if you think of anything else, don't hesitate to call again. Goodnight."

The following morning, the policeman spent three hours going over and over three different files. The first one contained notes and tapes taken from his long meetings with the old actor in Paraguay, together with notes his mother remembered about the man. The second file was material from his two interviews with Otto Skorzeny, and the third one contained transcriptions of his most recent tapes from Buenos Aires. There had to be a connection. Somewhere, there had to be that elusive common thread. The U-Boat was most certainly the key.

He closed the files and buzzed his secretary. "Get Volker and Schneider in here right away. Tell them to drop whatever they are doing."

Five minutes later, both his curious assistants came in, were told to sit, and then heard their new orders. "Whatever you're working on now, shelve it. I have a more important job for you." He smiled at forty year-old Friedrich Volker first. "Sorry, Friedrich, but your leave is cancelled. I promise to make it up to you. You are to find out everything you can about the World War II U-Boat hero, Korvettenkapitan Horst von Hellenbach. Research his family, his love life, his career, boats he commanded or served in, a list of any crew members who served with him—especially any who may still be alive.

"In short, everything. I want to know if he had blue or brown eyes. Whether he liked beer or wine. I need to know which hand he used to scratch his ass. In other words, no detail is unimportant, so don't leave anything out."

He shot a frosty look at Willi Schneider. "Willi, I want you to contact the British and the Americans. You know the right people to talk to. I need to find out if any German U-Boats were sunk or captured between the last week of April and the date of their surrender in 1945, and if so, where. You may start right now. Dismissed."

Both of his loyal officers hurried out. Neither had asked the first question, nor had they argued about breaking into work already in progress. The policeman had not given them a deadline either, knowing they would be professionally thorough, and would produce the requested information rapidly as humanly possible.

He was reaching for his file on Martin Bormann's wife and family when the black telephone rang. "Yes?"

"This is Johnny again. I have finally relocated the subject."

"It's about time. I thought when he left the Mayo Clinic in Minnesota, he went back to New York."

"He did."

"Don't tell me you lost him there."

"I'm sorry. He went south by car. How was I to know his manager was going to drive him?"

"Drive him where?"

"To an island off the North Carolina coast."

"*Which* island, Johnny?"

"Roanoke Island. A small town called Manteo. He has taken a house there. I think he has left New York for good."

"Don't lose him again, and keep me informed."

"You got it."

The policeman replaced the phone, got up and walked to a shelf that contained, among other reference books, an up to date world atlas. It took him only a moment or two to locate Roanoke Island. He studied the map for a few minutes more, and went back to his desk. He opened the Bormann family file again, allowing himself a snide snicker. Alois Manfred von Bittnerhof was not the only rat who had left a wife and family behind.

Not to mention a mistress.

◆

Chapter 8

Those days of June and the first half of July were like an unbroken string of precious pearls; each one a newly discovered gem to be treasured, and which Dieter made notes like amateurish love songs of in his diary while Susan slept. His preparations for Dr. Lert's workshop, no longer all-consuming, were squeezed into the morning hours until lunch and evening hours after dinner while Suzi (as he now called her) worked at the restaurant. The afternoon hours, weekends, and days she took off from work, were spent on her motorcycle, exploring the Outer Banks. Dieter repressed telling her, when she gushed on and on like a rip tide about the two hundred-year old history of the Banks, that historical periods of his own country were measured not in hundreds of years, but thousands.

Even so, his appreciation for the unusual geographical phenomenon and the colorful history of its people grew, and he began to somehow feel a part of it all. They had started at the northernmost part, near the Virginia line, and had worked their way, over time, down the northern half of the two hundred-mile length of those thin barrier islands which physically had changed so much over the millennia, and were still changing. Like osmosis, the significance of the string of islands--relative to the interior--seeped into Dieter's brain. He began to understood how amazing this part of the world was; a sand reef pushed up by the ocean, creeping westward a few inches per year toward the mainland it protects from storms, the fury of the Atlantic, and in the past, unwanted invaders. Suzi explained how that prehistorically, it might have been one continuous dune, and how tremendous pressure of inland waters from the rivers and sounds breached it from time to time, in different places, causing inlets (which rightly should be termed outlets) to be formed. These opened and closed at the whim of nature, and there was nothing man could do about it, although many had tried.

Suzi pointed out how weather and early ignorance of preservation methods had caused entire forest areas and grazing lands to literally disappear, overrun by advancing sand and supplanted with a steady buildup of man-made houses, settlements, and villages. The inhabitants, who were descendants of early Virginia settlers, herdsmen, runaways, fishermen and whalers, scratched out an existence from what was left—the ocean, the sounds, and later, the tourists.

In those six weeks, they rushed up, then down the coastline from the quaint villages of Corolla and Duck all the way to Ocracoke on the North Banks, stopping in each of the areas of interest in between; Kitty Hawk, Colington, Nags Head, and further down, Rodanthe, Waves, Salvo, Avon, and Buxton, with Suzi relating to him, in various restaurants or resting on one beach or another, their numerous--and humorous--stories. Dieter learned of Old

Quork, the Seven Sisters, how Nags Head and Jockey Ridge came by their names, the Pirates' Lights, and, on Ocracoke Island, all he ever wanted to know about the pirate, Blackbeard.

At home at Manteo, after making love in One-eyed Rosie's Victorian bedroom, Suzi would tell him, in childlike whispers, the pretty romance of the Ghost Deer of Roanoke, one of the many folk-legends which have grown up around the mysterious disappearance of Virginia Dare, the first English child born in the Colonies, her parents, and the rest of those unfortunate first colonists. Dieter loved everything she showed and told him, because he loved *her*. She was part of it, and to share it all with him was simply sharing another important part of herself.

They discussed the race "problem" only once. One Saturday night, they had walked to the Dairy Queen for an ice-cream cone, and on the way back, Dieter casually asked her to tell him something about her parents.

"I will, someday. Not right now, Dieter."

"Why not now?"

"Because this summer, at least so far, has been perfect. I don't want anything to spoil it."

Dieter decided not to press. Instead, he asked, "You miss being in the pageant this year? I feel a little guilty for taking you away from it."

Suzi laughed. "Lord, no. Prancing around in ways real Indian girls never would have? No way. The only reason I ever did that in the first place was to hope to meet a prince charming type who would carry me away from Roanoke Island in his white Cadillac."

"You mean the professional cast members? I'm surprised no one did."

"Oh, plenty tried, all right. Only, most of them were Yankees and had moves like frogs, not princes. All they wanted was to get in my pants. Plus, if any man-jack of them--who wasn't gay--really was half way interested in me as a person, he'd run the other way fast when one or another of the cast told him I was black, and had a mother who looked like an African Queen."

The ice cream had been finished when they reached Rosie's porch. They sat on the steps, and Dieter said, "Suzi, I really don't understand. If your mother was black and your father white, why can't you be either white or black?"

"Watch out, Dieter, your German logic is showing."

"That may be, but why don't *you* have the choice?"

"Haven't you ever heard of the one-drop syndrome?"

"The what?"

The one-drop syndrome. If you're tainted with one drop of black blood in you, you're black. Period."

"Suzi, excuse me, but this is 1979, not—"

"No, it's true. Still true. The degree doesn't matter. You can be one half, one quarter, one sixteenth black, but you're still black. I don't want to talk about it any more right now. Some other time, maybe. I know you're not like the rest of them, Sugar. That's enough for me. Look, I have tomorrow off. Where would you like to go?"

"I'd like to go back to the lighthouse at Cape Hatteras. There's something there in the museum I want to see, but the first time we went there, I didn't take the time."

"Okay. Mama says that lighthouse is going to fall into the ocean pretty soon if they don't do something about the beach erosion."

That particular problem was not what Dieter had been thinking about, and Suzi's comment, on top of what they had just talked about, reminded him that they had spent the last several days and nights together. Suzi had not been to her trailer house at all except to pick up what clothes she needed. Nor had she taken Dieter back there with her. Until now, he hadn't even wondered why.

"Haven't you talked to your parents about us?"

Suzi squirmed. Dieter could sense he had asked the wrong question. She sighed, and dropped her eyes as she replied, "Not yet. They sometimes spend weeks at the time offshore. I'll get around to it. What is it you want to see at the lighthouse?"

"Just one of the exhibits there, but what I want most of all is to go back to Pea Island for another midnight swim."

This suggestion changed her expression entirely. She looked up, smirked, and said, "Think we ought to take bathing suits this time?"

"What for? Chances are there won't be any more people there than before."

"Well, fine. But this time, we can take some towels and a blanket. That sand has a way of getting in all the wrong places, Mr. Sex Maniac."

The following day, Dieter received a form letter from the office of the American Symphony Orchestra League, explaining what he should bring to the three-week-long stay at Dr. Lert's Orkney Springs workshop in western

Virginia, along with a map of how to get there. He gave the letter a cursory reading, and laid it on top of the dresser. He and Suzi ate a late breakfast, climbed on the red Kawasaki, and rode back down to Cape Hatteras.

There was already a sizable crowd of camera-clicking tourists milling about, but they moved through them into the well-kept wood-frame house adjacent to the lighthouse, which served as both a curio shop and museum. Dieter took Suzi's hand and led her upstairs to the exhibit he'd noticed there before but had not taken the time to study. It was a collection of artifacts and photographs of the awesome World War II German submarine warfare off the North Carolina coast which had sent so many vessels to the Graveyard of the Atlantic. Hitler's U-Boats had taken a staggering toll of shipping and life, mostly during the years of 1942-43, with practically no losses to themselves.

Dieter seemed lost in thought. He stood there as in a trance until Suzi squeezed his hand and said, "Funny, one time, when I was a kid, I saw Daddy stare at that stuff the same way you are now. What's so interesting about it? That was a long time ago. Before we were born."

Dieter said nothing in reply, until they had gone back downstairs and sat on one of the wooden porch benches. "Suzi, my father was Captain of one of those German submarines."

"Really? Come to think of it, you haven't said anything at all to me about your own family, Dieter. Want to talk about it?"

He shrugged. "Why not? I never knew my father. He was lost at sea. Killed in action less than a month before the war ended and several months before I was born. My mother married my father's brother less than a year later."

"I'm sorry, Sugar."

"Don't be. I'm glad I never knew him."

"Dieter! Why would you say such a thing?"

Dieter took both her hands in his. "You *should* be able to understand it, Suzi, considering your own background, I mean, growing up with the race problems and all. My father was considered a war hero. A German war hero, but he was a Nazi. One of Hitler's faithful fanatics. So was his brother, my stepfather. I couldn't stand him either, and I hated what my father had been and what he had done. The sons and daughters of Nazis, my generation, had a lot to live down. We still do."

He was tempted to tell Suzi that was the primary reason why he had altered his name, but held back, realizing she probably would not have cared anyway. Besides, he was far too happy basking in the new sunshine of her love to allow any kind of past shadow to drift over it. Instead, he changed the subject completely. "Suzi, where can we rent a car?"

"A car? I don't know, somewhere in Nags Head, I guess. Why?"

"Because the workshop starts next week, and I want you to come with me."

"For three whole weeks? Are you sure? Wouldn't I be a... you know, kind of a distraction?"

Dieter giggled, leaned over and kissed her on her forehead. "I hope so, my love. I certainly hope so."

◆

Chapter 9

Nothing in Dieter's past traveling experience could have prepared him for the place he and Suzi were to live for those final weeks of July and the first week of August. When she drove up to the front of the "hotel" at Orkney Springs (which itself was literally at the end of the road) Dieter didn't know whether to laugh or cry. The monstrous four-story wooden structure had been an exclusive hot springs spa *before* the American Civil War, and had been used as a Confederate hospital during that war. It had since passed through the hands of a string of owners, each hoping to make a living from Washington area vacationers who wished to 'get away from it all' for a while. It was away from everything, all right. Twenty-five miles away from the nearest hint of a town!

While the location of the hotel and grounds was truly beautiful, nestled as it was in the gentle mountains that were the western slopes of the Shenandoah valley, the main building--and the collection of equally decrepit houses, cottages, and a quadrangular, two-story edifice containing perhaps eighty separate rooms--was not to be believed! They looked like little more than stalls of a stable, and none looked as though they had been repainted since the days of Lincoln's assassination.

At first glance, Dieter wondered aloud if a single match or malicious bolt of lightning would surely turn the entire collection into a gigantic bonfire, but Suzi thought not. "These buildings are like old wooden ships washed up on the beach. They're so waterlogged I doubt if they would burn even if you torched them. This whole place feels like a rain forest."

They walked up noisy steps and crossed a gap-planked porch, which sloped even more than Rosie's, and entered a huge lobby full of antiques, including two square grand pianos that most likely had not been played in a hundred years. The registration desk, located to the right of a grand staircase, looked like something straight out of a Charles Dickens novel, but was polished so that they could see their reflections in it. Dieter signed the register and held his hand out for their room key. The genial hostess, a plump lady in her mid-forties, merely laughed. "Oh, there aren't any keys here any more. Most of the doors are too warped to close tight, but you don't have to worry about security or privacy, believe me. Welcome to the village of Orkney Springs. I'm sure you and Mrs. Bach will enjoy your stay here."

Dieter let the "Mrs. Bach" comment pass, and Suzi kept a straight face.

A shriveled little man dressed in bib overalls materialized next to them, smiling and tipping the brim of a tattered straw hat. The hostess said, "Homer will show you to your room."

Homer--they never found out what his last name was--was the porter/handyman; ninety if he was a day, and could not have possibly carried anything heavier than a woman's purse. "Right this-a-way, folks. Just foller me." This took a while, since Homer's gait was somewhere between *largo* and *adagio*. Talking a mile a minute, he showed them into a room half way down the first floor of the quad, facing, across a macadam street, four of the cottages, which were as alike as four rusting mailboxes. The room was just large enough for a double bed, two rickety chairs, and a dresser—three knobs of its four drawers were missing. A brown-stained sink graced one corner, and the room had been made even smaller by a thin, paneled partition which sported two plywood doors; one leading to a tiny bathroom (tub/shower and toilet), the other opening into a mini-closet. The room smelled like a smuggler's cave. Suzi brought the car around and they unloaded clothes, Dieter's suitcase full of scores, and the linens and towels he had been advised to bring along. Suzi saw the look of utter dismay on his face, smiled and said, "I've seen worse, Dieter. Lots worse. Come on, let's have a look around."

The rough paved street in front of their room became a worn footpath leading to a muddy pond (the hot spring of another time?) guarded by an ornate gazebo whose latticework was as blanched as all the other buildings. As they got closer, Dieter heard some familiar music, and could not resist a smile when he saw the string quartet sawing away beneath the tin roof.

"What's that music?" Suzi wanted to know.

"One of the late Haydn quartets. Best not to disturb them. Look over there." He pointed to the right. "Is that what I think it is?" What they were looking at, fifty yards further down the path, was a modern, rather large swimming pool.

Suzi clapped her hands in delight. "A pool, Dieter! Can you believe it? Maybe this prison compound won't be so bad after all."

They walked down to the pool and tested the water. It was quite cold. (The next time they were to come down to it, three days later, they'd spot several cases of beer resting on its bottom—the best refrigerator in the entire enclave!)

A few yards up the slope from the pool was a shoddy tennis court, its net drooping in the middle like a sway-backed old dray horse. They would soon discover that no one used it for its intended purpose, but it made a fine spot for brass ensembles to blast away, downwind from everyone else. Suddenly Dieter understood everything. "It's brilliant, Suzi."

"What is?"

"The hotel. The whole place. Look, what we are supposed to do here is intense study. What could be better? It's miles away from ordinary distractions; no bars, no movie houses, no TV or even a radio unless you bring one with you. You can take long walks and maybe go swimming, but otherwise there is nothing here to take your mind off your work. It's perfect. Like that country place near Vienna where Beethoven used to spend his summers."

Suzi laughed. "I'll bet Beethoven didn't have a pool."

Dieter took her hand and started back toward the quad. "No. There was another thing he didn't have."

"What?"

"He didn't have you. I think I'm going to love Orkney Springs. Let's go back to the room and unpack."

They did, eventually. . .

And that night, at the cottage designated as the 'Conductors' House' Dieter met the other eleven conductors and the old man himself. They sat around a large table with Dr. Lert presiding from one end like King Arthur, beaming benevolently at his true Knights. He shook hands with each, and got right down to business. In his still strong Viennese accent he said, "This is an informal session. Tomorrow morning, and every morning after, we will meet here at eight for score study. There will be an afternoon and an evening rehearsal every day in the Lion Room, and each of you will conduct half-hour segments, which will be video-taped. This first week is devoted to chamber orchestra literature. The second and third weeks, we will have the full orchestra. Do any of you have any questions?"

No one did, and he went on. "Now, it would be nice if each of you would tell us something about yourself."

Each man, in turn, briefly said who they were, mentioned their orchestral affiliation, and why they had come. 'To become a better conductor' was the stock answer. Most of them were more or less Dieter's age, but many were already music directors of their own orchestras, or assistant conductors somewhere, and all had considerable professional experience. Dieter was embarrassed when his turn came, because he had no affiliation with any orchestra. Though each of the others maintained a neutral expression while he was speaking,

Dieter was certain that every single one of them knew who he was, what he had been, and why he was there.

"I am hoping to find out if I can learn to conduct effectively," he said honestly. There was absolutely no reaction from any of them, but Dieter was instantly seized with the sinking feeling that he was an interloper. A fish out of home waters.

Lert saved the moment. "Mr. Bach has had a distinguished career as a concert violinist, and his presence here shows a great deal of courage. We shall see if we can turn his bow into a baton."

Lert was, or rather, had been, a tall man. Age had bent his large frame into a kind of permanent stoop, which gave the appearance of his being tilted forward and a little to one side. His hands, which rested on the table, were massive, and steady as a rock, as was his gaze, but his eyes and smile were warm. Dieter would quickly discover that Lert was possessed of a wonderful sense of humor, yet one that could often turn brutal when something provoked him. He winked privately at Dieter, and went on to the next man.

The rest of the evening was social. Coffee was served, and when Lert moved upstairs to his apartment, taking with him the tension of that initial session, everyone present relaxed into a congenial gathering of colleagues. In the space of one hour, Dieter heard many of the horror stories of past workshops, found that Lert had been in the same class with Otto Klemperer and Erich Kleiber, had been married to Vicki Baum, the German novelist who had written *GRAND HOTEL* -- and had escaped Nazi Germany when Hollywood decided to make a movie of that work --

and was supposedly related (Nephew) to Brahms himself. Dieter didn't know whether any or all of that was true, but found himself wanting to believe all of it, just like all the other men there; each man reverently saying how lucky they all were to study with a living legend.

The following morning, Dieter had his baptism. After a breakfast, which was indescribable, he found himself back at the table with his assigned scores in front of him. Lert looked at the first man to his left. "Tell us how you study a score, please."

As each man around the table confidently told the Master how he prepared a score for rehearsal and performance, Dieter began to feel very uncomfortable. He could scarcely believe some of the ridiculous "methods" some of those men described, ranging from playing each part of an orchestral score on their own instruments; piano, violin, or whatever, to totally formal academic analysis! As each conductor finished, the smile left Lert's face, replaced by a scowl, which deepened as the next man tried to top the one before. When his turn came: "Mr. Bach, how do you study a score?" Dieter's face turned apple red while he stammered, "I simply listen to it."

Unrestrained laughter broke out all around the table, and Dieter's humiliation was complete. But Richard Lert was not laughing. He merely nodded at Dieter and mercifully went on to the next man. Salvation came at the end of that particular part of the session. One of the other men blatantly asked, "Dr. Lert, how do *you* study a score?"

Lert chuckled and answered right away, "Why, it's easy. Whether it is a little piece of four-part music like Mozart's *Nachtmusik*, which each of you will conduct, or a complex score by Richard Strauss or Mahler, I study it one measure at a time. When I know the first measure, I go on to the next."

They could have heard the proverbial pin drop. Dieter could never remember seeing so many long faces in one room. Then, Lert surprised them all. "Mr. Bach, you said you study a score by listening to it. Could you sing the first violin part of the Mozart for us?"

Lert stopped Dieter after only a few measures, and then asked him to sing the bass part. Dieter obeyed, and was stopped again, after only a few bars, then asked if he could sing the viola part. Once more Dieter managed several measures before Lert stopped him, then looked around the table and said, "Gentlemen, Mr. Bach has sung very accurately, and in the key of G Major. Apparently, he listens quite well, doesn't he? And perfect pitch is a blessing in our profession."

His eyes rested on Dieter once again, and in a soft tone, he said, "Mr. Bach, we realize you have not had much experience in conducting, but you have great experience in performing. Tell me, what do you think would be the most difficult music to conduct?"

The moment Dieter gave his answer, he knew with certainty that the old man was helping him over a big hurdle with the others—regarding respect. "I think the hardest thing for a conductor is accompanying soloists."

Lert grinned. He looked around the table and said, "He's right, you know. If you don't believe it, try conducting an opera. Singers are the absolute worst. Let's have a short break, now."

There was a general rush to the outside door and the men gathered in two groups, smokers and non-smokers, all chattering like wives at a card party, confused at Lert's reaction to their over-confidant answers. Dieter stood nervously on the fringe and listened. No one spoke to him for the first few minutes, then, one of Lert's two assistants, a pleasant fellow named Jones, walked up and shook hands. "Dr. Lert," he said with a warm smile, "Is as good a psychologist as he is a conductor. Have you ever heard the old saying—give a man enough rope to hang himself?"

"Yes, I have. I think I understand what you're getting at. He doesn't like smart alecks."

"Exactly. He values sincerity above everything. We are all babes in the woods compared to his experience and knowledge. He doesn't care one bit whether we know very much or not, only whether we have the ability to learn."

"I can see that. You've worked with him a lot?"

"Several years, and he still often treats me like a wet-behind-the-ears kid. The trick with him is to simply be yourself. Make your mistakes, take your medicine, and go on from there. You'll be fine."

"Thanks. I hope you're right."

Later, in the bed which rolled them both to its middle, Dieter told Suzi everything that had happened, whispering, because he was certain a normal conversation could be heard through at least two or three of the thin walls in both directions. "—And I'm going to conduct tomorrow night for the first time. Keep your fingers crossed."

Beneath the clammy sheet, Suzi squeezed his hand. "Like that Jones guy said, just be yourself. You'll be fine. Can I come and watch?"

◆

Chapter 10

Rehearsals were held in the hotel's old grand ballroom, which was nicknamed the "Lion room" because of a gigantic, framed painting of a full-grown, but sleepy male lion which hung on the wall directly behind the podium. The setup for the small orchestra seemed miniscule in the room, which opened out onto a spacious balcony, not through doors, strangely enough, but through several proportionately large windows. Lert sat on a raised platform next to the podium, close enough to whichever conductor who was working to touch his elbow, or say something softly to him.

It became apparent to Dieter half way through the first session that the reason Lert chose the small orchestra to begin the conductor sessions was to evaluate the basic podium skills of each man; baton technique, how good an ear the men had, whether they chose the correct tempo for whatever piece they were working on, and whether they had some idea of its style. He said very little to any of them.

After that first rehearsal, he called Dieter over and said, "Mr. Bach, this year we happen to have two outstanding violinists in the orchestra. I'm going to change your first assignment because of it. Come, walk back to my house with me."

Dieter had no idea what Lert had in mind or what to say. When they reached the conductors' house, he was told to take a seat, and Lert disappeared upstairs. He returned a moment later with a score in his hand, which he handed to Dieter. It was the *Concerto for Two Violins* by J.S. Bach. "Have you played this before?"

"Yes, sir. Many times. Both solo parts."

"I thought as much. I'd like for you to conduct this tonight instead of the Schubert. Would you mind?"

"No, sir. Not at all," Dieter answered, his mind racing like a runaway train, full of wild speculation as to why Lert had made this decision.

The Master quickly eased Dieter's budding apprehension."I thought this piece might be a better one for you to start out with. You should feel comfortable with it. We probably won't have time to do more than the first two movements, but it might be fun for you."

And it was. The concertmaster and the assistant concertmaster played very well, and Dieter found himself "playing chamber music" along with them, giving no conscious thought whatsoever to the wooden stick in his right hand. Together, they found a good tempo, and the little concerto went rolling along quite nicely, as if it had a life and will of its own, and when Dieter's half-hour segment was over, he was convinced Richard Lert was a genius. By casting him back into familiar waters, Lert had made it easy for him to pass his first test. Dieter had not been aware of actually conducting, *per se,* rather, it was as though he and the other players were a third violin, meshing their counterpoint with those of the two soloists. Lert said not a word, but the players began their foot-shuffling; the age-old traditional signature of orchestral approval, and Dieter knew that with them at least, he had made a good start.

After lunch the following day, he sat down with Lert's assistant and watched the videotape of his segment, astounded at what he saw. On the podium, he'd seemed relaxed, smiled often, and had made no obtrusive or unnecessary gestures. Jones stopped the machine, looked at him with a grin and said. "Can you tell me what the best part was?"

Dieter didn't know what he meant, and said so.

"You didn't look down at the score one single time! The players were following your eyes as much as they were your baton. It was real orchestral communication, Dieter. Fine job. Keep it up."

Two days later, Dieter conducted the first two movements of Mozart's *Nachtmusik*, with much the same results. It was a heady experience, as was the sudden friendliness of most of the orchestra players, who came to him afterwards to shake his hand. The other conductors were cool. More and more distant, which saddened Dieter, but there seemed little he could do about it.

Suzi was enjoying herself immensely. The whole Orkney Springs package was a great adventure for her, each rehearsal a tremendous learning experience, and she suffered little from the growing snobbish attitude of other conductor's wives or girlfriends, having quickly grasped the reasons for the inevitable petty jealousies none too subtly hinted at around the dining tables and the pool. The Orkney "musical family" was like any other large family. Minor squabbles were unavoidable, but she and Dieter were too much in love and too happy about what was happening to spend any time worrying about silly attitudes, which were out of their control anyway. In the end, Suzi's looks and vibrant personality largely overcame most of it, and they both made friends who would, they were sure, become permanent ones.

The first rehearsal of the full orchestra was a literal revelation. With his own eyes (and ears) Dieter witnessed a kind of musical miracle. Lert himself traditionally conducted the first segment of the opening session; always with the same work, Wagner's Prelude to *Die Meistersinger*. Dieter and Suzi sat behind the huge orchestra on the sill of one of the big windows and watched as the old man raised his baton and brought it down forcefully. The C-Major chord of the first measure erupted like a cannon shot. His left hand never moved from his side. Only the stick in his right hand and his blazing eyes were in motion. The first two or three minutes, the orchestra sounded horrible. So much so, Dieter found himself holding his breath. Lert never stopped them. Gradually, Dieter saw and heard, and therefore understood, what conducting was all about. By sheer force of will, and total knowledge of every facet of the music, Lert brought the massive forces under submission. Attacks became sharp. Ragged passages became clearer. Orchestral balance grew more homogenous. Phrasing became tasteful. In short, it was like an animal trainer taming a wild beast before his very eyes and ears. By the time the final measures thundered forth, Lert had the entire orchestra under complete control, and before the piece ended, sounding like an ensemble that had played together for years! When the echoes finally died out, he smiled at them, and said, "Thank you. You are a good orchestra."

Dieter instantly had a distinct feeling of gratitude that he was not the unfortunate fellow who had to follow that session!

The fact was, he did not get a chance to conduct a single note during the entire first week. Suzi asked, "Why not?"

"I don't know, my love. In the first place, Lert never assigned me any of the large orchestral repertoire. He must have his reasons."

The morning of the second day of that third week, though Dieter was not to realize it until afterwards, he saw why Jones had called Lert a master psychologist. They were at the square table in the middle of score study. The particular piece on the table was the "Italian" Symphony of Mendelssohn. Two conductors in consecutive sessions had worked like Trojans on the first movement, and could not figure out why the playing had been bad. Awful, in fact. So rough that Lert had nearly lost his temper with the two nervous conductors who had tried their best. The harder they had worked, the worse it had sounded, until both had been flailing away hopelessly. Lert was practically beside himself and was trying his own best to get someone around the table to pinpoint the problem.

He suddenly fell silent, drummed his fingers on the table, and then sharply looked at Dieter. "What's wrong with it, Bach?"

Dieter felt every eye, many of them hostile, on him and quickly surmised Lert was giving him the opportunity to pass or fail his second test. He took a deep breath and said, "It's too heavy."

"Explain."

"Well, I remember so many times playing the Mendelssohn Violin Concerto. For the orchestra, and the conductor, there is never much of a problem until the last movement, which is so fast and so light, it is impossible to give two beats per measure. It makes the concerto ponderous. Heavy. I think this symphony is the same. It should be conducted in one to the bar, if that."

"Would you mind trying it tonight?"

"I can try. Yes sir."

"Good. Now, what's next here?"

That evening, Suzi perched on their familiar window-sill seat, gazing confidently at her lover. Dieter mentally counted three measures, lifted his stick for the fourth, and brought it down the way one might pat a bird on its head. The A-Major chord of the two-measure introduction chirped forth cleanly, and Dieter had only to glance at the violins and the melody of the first theme sang out like a prisoner released from jail. The entire movement sailed along like a fast catamaran on a broad reach, and Dieter found that he only had to touch spots in the air with the tip of the baton to control it all. It was like the first glass of good champagne, and he enjoyed it much the same way.

It was over before he knew it, and the foot-shuffling this time included several quite audible thumps of heels on the floor. Lert nodded at him, smiled once, and said, "Now, this was all much better. Fine. Go on to the next movement, please."

Dieter had to catch his mental breath before starting that stately piece, but had just enough time to finish it before the time was up, again using a light baton. He got another half-smile from the old man, and made his way to Suzi's side, knowing he'd made one hundred friends and two bitter enemies within the space of thirty minutes!

"You did good, didn't you," Suzi whispered as the concertmaster rose to re-tune the orchestra.

"I think so."

"You did. Even I could tell. We need to celebrate tonight."

"Where?"

"You'll see."

Somewhere, Suzi had found a pair of candles which lent a much more romantic shadow-light than did the single un-shaded bulb which hung from the ceiling by its own cord. They had begun slowly undressing each other when they heard a discreet knock on the door. Knowing there was no lock, they froze in place, near panic, then frantically scrambled to retrieve scattered garments and put them back on while Dieter yelled, "Just a moment!" Suzi also spoke a single word, and Dieter found himself praying she had not said it loud enough for whoever was standing at the door to hear! He switched the overhead light on, blew out the candles and opened the door.

His embarrassment and anger were replaced by surprise and total bewilderment when he saw Sy Glazer and Dr. Lert standing there, trying hard to suppress grins. Sy spoke first. "May we come in, Dieter? We need to talk."

Dieter glanced once at Suzi, whose eyes looked like a pair of cymbals, then found his voice. "Of course. Please."

Lert and Sy took the two chairs. Suzi sat stiffly on the edge of the mussed bed. Dieter was too nervous to sit.

Sy began. "I flew to Washington this morning and rented a car. Thought I'd never find this place. Anyway, Dr. Lert and I have had a long discussion, and, well, I think he'd best tell you himself."

Lert removed the black beret he wore everywhere, gave Suzi the warmest of glances, looked at Dieter and said, "Young man, I didn't tell you before, but I heard you play with Mehta in Los Angeles three years ago, and when I decided to have you come here, I took the trouble to listen to all of your recordings."

Dieter felt his face heating up.

The old man leaned forward. "In my mind, there never was any question about your musicianship, and you have handled the awkward situation here very well. I knew I would not have to coach you on matters like style and tempo. I knew you already had a fine sense of orchestral balance, and your ear is perfect. My biggest concern for you was to find out if you could transfer all of that into baton work. You have shown that you can. Naturally, there is room for improvement, but that will come in time. I have purposefully kept you off the podium, knowing you would watch every man closely. No better way to learn what to do technically, and better yet, what not to do.

"In short, there is no question in my mind that you can become a first rate conductor, perhaps a most outstanding one, and have said as much to Mr. Glazer here. I have also made a few suggestions to him regarding the next steps I think you should take." He looked at Sy, as if to say, 'Continue, please.'

Dieter began to feel weak in the knees, and sat down beside Suzi on the bed.

"Put it this way, Dieter," Sy said. "I could get you guest dates with several of the big orchestras, both here and in Europe. Most of them would be glad to have you guest conduct, based on your past reputation and fame as a violinist, but you'd be like a novelty. Dr. Lert thinks that would not be the best way to go right now, and after hearing his reasoning, I have to agree. What he pointed out makes a lot of sense, which is this: Orchestras in New York, Chicago, Philly, you know, the big ones, can all play perfectly, no matter who stands in front of them. Dr. Lert thinks you should get some experience with some of the, well, lesser orchestras. Help me out here, Dr. Lert."

The old man looked up at Dieter, his face now deadly serious. "You need experience *rehearsing*, Dieter. Rolling up your sleeves and getting your hands dirty fixing mistakes, correcting wrong notes, intonation problems, bad phrasing, poor balance. All brass sections play too loud, you know.

"You need to learn how to take a piece of music apart, then put it back together again. Shape it, and shape the orchestra, then work on building repertoire. You will also need to fashion your own interpretations, much as you already have the concerto repertoire. I think that part will not be difficult for you. Nevertheless, I think it would be good for you to work with the smaller orchestras first, maybe take one of them for a year or two as music director, and in between, accept a few dates with some of the major orchestras.

"You are lucky to have an agent like Mr. Glazer. Most of the other men here would gladly kill to have such an advantage, but then, most of them will not get very far, and would not-- even if they had Simon Peter for an agent. That's why most of them resent your being here."

"Does any of this make sense, Dieter?" Sy wanted to know.

"Yes. All of it does," Dieter managed.

Lert went on. "You have great gifts, son, not the least of which is a certain humility before the music. The players all sense that, and will therefore play their hearts out for you. I probably don't need to tell you this, but I will anyway. Right here and now, I'm going to give you the three most important keys to success as a conductor. First, if you want to make great music with any orchestra, no matter whether it be the Berlin Philharmonic or the South New Mexico Symphony, never distance yourself from them or hold your hands up to them in an arrogant manner. Always take the orchestra in your arms. I agree with the fellow who said there are no bad orchestras, only bad conductors. Second, and this is very important. You can always lead a group of musicians, but you can never drive them. They want simple leadership, not a condescending know-it-all musicologist tyrant. And third, while rehearsing, let your stick do most of the talking.

"I hope you will come back here next summer, and if you can manage it, come to me in California from time to time. There are a lot of tricks of the trade, as they say, that

I would like to show you, and I don't know how much time I have left."

"I would like nothing better, Dr. Lert, believe me," Dieter stammered.

"Good. Only one other thing." He glanced at Suzi with a mischievous grin. "If you bring this charming young lady with you, I'll do my best to take her away from you!"

Dieter fell in love with Suzi all over again when she jumped up, ran to Lert, kissed him on the cheek, and said, "And you'd be the only one who ever could, Dr. Lert."

There was little more of conversation. Lert said something about getting back to his house before his "keepers" missed him and sent out a search party, and Sy said he would return to New York first thing in the morning, hoping he would get back to Washington before he starved to death, and that he would be in touch. They had not been gone more than five minutes when Suzi re-lit the candles and, puncturing the silent vacuum, said, "We're a long way from Pea Island, Mr. Conductor, but don't you think we can imagine we're there?"

Dieter could. Most of the night. . .

What remained of their time at Orkney Springs flew past like bits and pieces of dreams remembered. Before they knew it, they were saying their good-byes to everyone, including Homer, who gallantly offered to help them pack the car, actually carried two pillows to it, and graciously accepted Dieter's over-generous tip.

They joined the outbound caravan, joking about being full-fledged 'Orks;" having survived the crucible of Lert's workshop, the abominable food, and the sagging bed-- and had the bed-bug bites to prove it. The elation at Dieter's unexpected good fortune—and future prospects--was so alive inside him, he asked Suzi to stop the car at the first sizeable town, where he found a jewelry shop, asked Suzi to marry him while standing at its door, and when she said she would, took her inside and bought her a diamond ring big enough to max out his credit card.

The rest of their trip back to Manteo should have been tiring, but was not, since the whole of it was consumed with joyous vocal speculation about their future together.

Dieter was grateful Suzi drove a car as well as she rode a motorcycle, and when they finally crossed the Croatan Sound, realized he was to shortly meet Suzi's mother and father, but had no inkling what an extraordinary woman Sunday Everette was and had been. Neither did he have any idea he would also come face to face with a living ghost from Adolf Hitler's Third Reich.

◆

Chapter 11

Suzi decided she wanted to have her parents come to Sophie's house for mid-day dinner; a traditional 'mess of fried fish, collards, sweet potatoes, and cornbread', which she felt would no doubt put them into a mood more receptive to hearing the news of her engagement and tentative marriage plans. Who was Dieter to argue with such logic? Soon, the kitchen was an olfactory rainbow. Ambivalent as he was about food, Dieter merely enjoyed watching his future wife bustle around the large room while reciting yet another Roanoke Island history lesson. This was a lengthy account of how there had been, directly after the American Civil War, an actual attempt by the occupying government to set up a negro colony on the island. Manteo had been the landing place for so many escapees and newly-freed blacks; men, women, and children. That audacious plan had almost worked! Streets, lots, and houses had been laid out and built, a school established, and a church erected.

That grand experiment had failed, unfortunately, but over time, both blacks and whites of Manteo had settled into routines of common work, life next to each other, and mutual respect which has lasted until the present. Not more than a few blocks away was the still-standing Free Will Holiness Church which Sunday attended faithfully when not at sea, and would walk to the house as soon as this morning's service was over. Charlie, she continued, never went to church, though he had no objections for Sunday to belong and attend, usually driving her to and from in a pickup truck Suzi said was older than sin itself. Charlie, she said, was never one to be idle. He always had plenty of boat work and net mending to do while they were gone.

"Do you ever go?" Dieter asked.

"Once in a while. I'll have to take you with me one morning, Sugar. It's pretty, well, colorful, no pun intended."

Suddenly, Suzi stopped stirring, sat down at the table across from him and said, "Dieter, I think I'd better tell you this now, before they come. My Daddy doesn't talk."

"You mean he's a quiet type?"

"No, I mean he *can't* talk. His jaw and throat were hurt a long time ago, and he has no use of his vocal chords. Years ago he and Mama developed a kind of shorthand Morse code system. Fast, too. Daddy hears very well, but he can't speak. I meant to tell you that earlier, but with everything that's been happening, I never got around to it. It's no big deal, but you'll have to be patient while Mama sort of translates anything he wants to say."

Dieter took a few moments to digest this news, and asked, "Suzi, how much have you told them about us? About me?"

"Nothing, except that I've fallen in love with a great looking white guy who is a musician named Dieter Bach."

"That's all?"

"What else could I have said? That was before we went to Orkney Springs."

"And they just accepted that?"

Suzi got up to stir the collards. "Sure. They know I've had boyfriends before, but they also know I never loved any of them. Till you."

She shooed Dieter out of the kitchen and Sophie's formal dining room, and with nothing better to do, he went into the living room, sat down, and extracted the letter he'd received the day before from Sy.

Dieter,

Please don't be offended by this, but I feel I must speak my mind.

Your phone call the other night put me into a cold sweat. The girl is certainly a knockout, and bright, but what on earth could you two have in common, aside from the obvious physical attraction? From what you said, she knows next to nothing about music, or what it would be like being married to a conductor. She's a *waitress,* for God's sake. Think of the social implications down the road! Frankly, I think it would be a terrible mistake for you to be married to anybody at this point in your career, and I beg you to reconsider this decision. You have never met my own son, who lives with his mother (my first wife) but I would give him the same advice, believe me.

Sincerely,

Sy G.

That was the only time Dieter could ever remember getting angry with Sy. He jammed the letter back into his pocket, resolving to destroy it, and never mention it to Suzi. Once he came to really know her, Dieter was certain Sy would adore her as much as he did. In any case, he didn't have time to brood about it. Within half an hour, there was a knock on the front door.

Sunday Everette was by far the most striking female member of the human species Dieter had ever seen. She was wearing high-heeled shoes, which subtracted nothing from her height, which was at least six feet. Nor did the pink flower-print summer dress she was wearing hide the fact that her figure was almost as good as Suzi's, but looked like it was all muscle—from head to toe. Hers was a body of both power and bearing. With skin the color of fine Swiss chocolate, she really *did* look like an African Queen. When she smiled, and she did right away, she showed twin rows of perfect, snow-white teeth, and her large brown eyes, also so much like Suzi's, seemed to Dieter to be ambassadors of good will. Turning slightly, she said, "This is my man, Charlie."

Her "man Charlie" was perhaps half an inch shorter. His hand, when he reached it out to shake Dieter's, was rough. Callused. No two fingernails were the same length, and his handshake, had he tried to, could have crushed Dieter's right one all over again. His eyes were light blue, set in a face that wind and sun had burned into the color of saddle leather. His iron-gray hair was cut short, and his smile, though friendly enough, was warped by the old injury Suzi had mentioned. In fact, the awful scar and indentation, which ran from his left cheekbone to his jaw, did not completely distort what had once been very handsome features. They certainly were not those of a common seaman, though his body, which was nearly bursting out of the badly fitting blue suit he wore, and his bowlegged gait testified that he was a man used to hard physical work, and one who had spent a great part of his life on a rolling deck.

When they all sat down to eat, Dieter couldn't help but notice that both Charlie and Sunday employed quite cultured table manners. This surprised him, though he couldn't have said why. Too, Charlie had brought three bottles of a decent white wine, which also surprised him, but it certainly helped him digest the mountain of southern food Suzi heaped on his plate.

As hostess, Suzi was in her element. Dieter was also proud of what a grasp of the musical chemistry she had absorbed at Orkney Springs, and how well she explained it to her parents, along with hilarious descriptions of how and where they'd lived for three weeks. She had no compunction at all in telling Sunday and Charlie that they had been, in essence, living under the same roof since practically the first day they had spent together, nor did she seem to expect any kind of objection or disapproval from them. Losing no opportunity to show off her new ring, she chattered away throughout the meal, as if she and Dieter had already been a married couple for twenty years! For his part, Dieter said very little, except to eventually ask them both to tell him their story after dinner.

And during those after dinner hours that stretched well into the evening he listened to the most fascinating tale he had ever heard! From the humble beginnings of her life and childhood, Sunday's story, which she told with such modesty--and honesty--nearly brought tears to Dieter's eyes. While she talked, Dieter stole glances at Suzi. Though she must have heard it all a hundred times before, she sat curled up next to him on the horsehide sofa like a worshipful spaniel, listening carefully and proudly to every word. Dieter never once interrupted, except to ask, "How did you and Charlie meet?"

Sunday gave Charlie a look of pure adoration, and said, "It happened during the last year of the war. I was out fishing one day, and found him floating on some wreckage. I figured he had been a sailor on some ship that got sunk, and I could see he was hurt pretty bad. I hauled him aboard my boat and brought him home.

"He had a bad cut on his head and his throat was messed up pretty bad, too. When he finally came around, he couldn't talk, and it took me a while to figure out he knew Morse. But that's all he knew. The bump on his head wiped out his memory. He couldn't even remember his name, let alone what ship he'd been in."

"Amnesia?"

"Yep. I called him Charlie, for lack of a better name, and that seemed to suit him all right." She reached over and squeezed his hand. "Didn't it?"

Charlie smiled and nodded.

"Anyway," Sunday continued, "It didn't take him long to get his health back, and I was happy as the dickens that he turned out to be one fine sailor man, and a real good fisherman to boot. We've been together ever since, and pretty successful, too. What with our fishing and my healing folks, we've done all right. Just in case you're wondering, I reckon God married us on my boat out in His Atlantic Ocean church, and Susan was born the next Christmas day. Since we never knew Charlie's last name, we just took mine. That's about it."

"What an amazing and wonderful story," Dieter said. "But what about your father? Slick. What did he think about it all?"

Sunday laughed lightly. "Oh, I guess he backslid again. Took off the day I brought Charlie home, and I never saw him again. He may be dead, for all I know. Probably is."

Charlie got up, poured some more wine, and blinked rapidly at Sunday, who then said, "Charlie wants to know more about you, Mr. Bach. Wants to know if you're descended from that famous family of musicians."

"No such luck," Dieter replied with a laugh of his own. "That's just a coincidence."

Whether it was the late hour, the large amount of wine he'd drunk, or a combination of the two, Dieter began talking before he knew it, thinking Suzi's mother and father certainly had every right to know more about the man who was going to marry their daughter. He told them basically what he'd already told Suzi, trying to underplay the reasoning for shortening his name. "It's actually--are you ready for this, Suzi?--Dieter Ernst von Hellenbach. I was named for my Grandfather. There are many personal reasons why, but mostly I felt that I would be more comfortable going through life simply as Dieter Bach."

Much later, Dieter thought that at that point in the conversation Sunday might have wanted to save him from any further awkward revelation. She broke in and said, "Well, Dieter Bach's a very fine name." She turned her head and gave Suzi a knowing look. "Since you two are going to get married, I might as well tell Dieter the part I left out. Ought not to be secrets in any family. She gave Dieter a soft look. "You see, back when I was about sixteen years old—"

What happened next caught Dieter completely by surprise. Charlie stood abruptly, flashed Sunday a rapid series of eye-messages, then turned on his heel and walked right out the front door, with Sunday only half a step behind him! Their sudden exit, so quick and unexpected, also bewildered Suzi, who froze in her position, speechless.

Dieter was suddenly angry. "What the devil was that all about? Did I say something wrong? Insulting?"

Suzi didn't answer him. Cursing softly, she got up and ran outside. Dieter followed her to the door to watch. He saw her run to the pickup, which was already backing out of the driveway, stand with her hands on her hips for a moment when it roared away, and then trudge back inside, still muttering. She took Dieter by the hand and led him to the sofa. "Sugar," she said, "That's the strangest damn thing I ever saw them do. I can't figure it out, unless—"

"Unless?"

"Unless Daddy was all of a sudden embarrassed about what Mama was going to tell you. Listen, I'm going to make this quick. When Mama was young, she cooked for a government work camp that stayed on Pea Island for a while. One of them was a black boy, a Doctor's son named George. Mama fell head over heels in love with him, but before things went too far, his Daddy came and got him.

Almost broke her heart. Not long after that, she was raped by four white boys who were part of the work gang. She got her revenge on them, though. The next day, she beat the living hell out of three of them and shot the ringleader in the crotch. His name was Bummy Keene. A real bastard.

"After the war was over, Keene came back. He had blackmailed George somehow and came back to Pea Island wanting his own revenge. He got the jump on Charlie and Amos, tied them up in the Station House, and tried to kill Mama *and* George. Charlie got free, and killed the son of a bitch, but not before he had set fire to Mama's shack. Charlie dived through a window and rescued both of them, George and Mama.

"Charlie and George were both burned pretty bad, but Mama healed them."

"Good God. How?"

Suzi smiled and stood. "She's a fire-talker. It's a gift she has. Look, I'll explain it all to you later. You stay here and wait for me. I'm going after them. Something tells me what I just told you isn't the whole reason they took off like that. It couldn't be."

She ran out, and Dieter watched her jump on her motorcycle, and tear off, burning rubber. He stood on the porch in a state of absolute stupefaction for a few minutes, and went back inside, to the kitchen to brew some strong coffee, thinking Suzi would be back within the hour. But she wasn't back in an hour. Or two. She did not return at all. Eventually, Dieter fell asleep on the sofa, too exhausted and dazed to try to think through any of it.

◆

Chapter 12

At first, Dieter thought he was dreaming. He'd left the lights on and when his eyes focused on Charlie's face, realizing strong hands were shaking him, he thought he had dreamed the entire scene of the night before—and it was continuing. But it was not a dream. Charlie Everette *was* standing there, this time dressed in a flannel shirt and faded jeans, a wool cap pulled down nearly to his eyes. Dieter looked at his watch, and at the same time, noticed the unmistakable smell of coffee coming from the kitchen. It was not yet six in the morning. His first conscious thought was embarrassment. Worse, dry mouth or not, he could not think of what to *say*. Should he call him Charlie? Mr. Everette? What? He sat up, shaking off the cobwebs, awake and aware enough at least to say nothing at all. Charlie brought him a mug of coffee, and handed him a note along with it:

PLEASE COME WITH ME. I MUST SHOW YOU SOMETHING IMPORTANT.

Dieter read the note, handed it back to him, and looked at his face. It was neither hard nor soft. Charlie was not smiling, but not frowning either. His face was neutral. It did not appear that he was angry, but Dieter knew this was something serious.

"All right, but may I wash my face first?"

Charlie nodded, still not changing his expression.

Dieter took a sip or two of the coffee, then got up and went to the bathroom, relieved himself, washed his hands and face and returned to the living room, but Charlie was not there. Dieter looked outside. Charlie was already waiting behind the wheel of his pickup which was parked at the curb, its motor running. Dieter had presence of mind to take the mug of hot coffee with him, and was lucky not to spill it when Charlie yanked the gearshift down, let out the clutch, and pulled away.

Fully awake now, Dieter managed not to ask Charlie where they were going, knowing he could not answer. Dieter would find out soon enough, he reasoned, wishing to God that Suzi—or Sunday—were sitting next to him.

Whether the antique truck was not capable of higher speed, or because Charlie was not in a big hurry, he drove no more than fifty over the causeway bridge, turned right, and down the length of Bodie Island as the sun rose like an orange bubble out of the Atlantic. Dieter finished the coffee long before they pulled into the parking lot of the Coast Guard Station and marina located on the north bank of Oregon Inlet. They left the truck and walked to the docks where several dozen sleek sport-fishing boats were moored. As they boarded one of them, a late-model Hatteras of around 45 feet, Dieter remembered something the Manteo barber had said; something about Charlie being a good charter captain. He also thought about the night Suzi had showed him the trawler, calling it "Mama's boat." Was this sport fisherman Charlie's boat? Charlie made no indication one way or the other, and went about the business of preparing to get underway with long-practiced, deliberate movements. If he needed or wanted Dieter's help, he didn't indicate it.

Dieter, naturally, said nothing, and waited until Charlie got the vessel out into the channel before meekly asking, "Are we going fishing?"

This idiotic question seemed to amuse Suzi's father. The hint of a smile worked its way around the corners of his mouth. For reply, he only shook his head and pointed northwest, toward Roanoke Island. Dieter's confusion only increased when, a short time later and after crossing the sound which looked like greasy dishwater, they pulled into the docks at Wanchese, on the opposite side of the pier from the trawler, whose name Dieter now noticed for the first time. In hand-painted black letters on both sides of her bow was: *BLACK DOLPHIN II*.

Sunday emerged from her cabin, folded her arms, gave Dieter a weak smile, and watched her common-law husband tie the yacht up, leaving the engines running. Charlie jumped to the dock, and as nimbly, hopped onto the trawler's deck, and both he and Sunday disappeared back into the cabin. Dieter remained where he was, wondering if Suzi was coming along with them. She was nowhere in sight, however, and her parents returned moments later, carrying an old-fashioned steamer trunk which they transferred to the deck of the yacht. Charlie straightened, then waited while Sunday went back for a plastic ice-chest which she handed over, and which he stowed on the afterdeck next to the trunk. If they had been, or still were, 'talking' to each other, Dieter couldn't tell, not being able to see their eyes.

Right away, Charlie ran forward, then aft, and caught the mooring lines Sunday threw him. Obviously, she was not coming along either. She waved once, and went back inside the trawler's cabin as they pulled away from the dock and headed into the channel. There was no traffic at all. If other trawlers were working, they would have left much earlier.

Charlie pointed to the seat opposite the helm, which Dieter silently took. Charlie preferred to stand, however, and shoved the throttles forward once they were in the main channel, and the boat sprang forward like a young Doberman on a tight leash. In what seemed no time at all, they were through the Oregon Inlet and into the open Atlantic, riding directly into the rising sun. The morning was absolutely gorgeous. Cloudless, and with only the slightest of swells. After a few minutes, Charlie set the auto-pilot, grabbed a pair of binoculars, and climbed to the flying bridge. Satisfied no one was in their path, he came back down, dragged the ice-chest between the captain's chairs, and opened it. Inside was enough food and drink for three days! Dieter's stomach suddenly reminded him he had consumed nothing but a cup of coffee, and he wasted no time digging into cold chicken and deviled eggs. There was beer, but he opted for a sealed jar of iced tea, which of course was very sweet. Charlie took a sandwich, a beer, and went up the flying bridge ladder again. This time Dieter followed.

They cruised east. Alone, seemingly, on the surface of the benign Atlantic. Dieter couldn't help but think this was the longest time he'd ever spent in the company of another person without a single word of conversation. It was altogether an eerie feeling, but since he didn't believe Charlie meant him any harm, the feeling of apprehension gradually gave way to simple curiosity.

They finished the impromptu breakfast just as they entered the shipping lanes. Dieter was astonished at the number of vessels in sight. Some small, some large, sailing basically north or south, and at good speed. Charlie changed course a number of times to give each of the vessels plenty of room, riding across wakes, which were sizable, even though their distance from the ships had to be as much as half a mile.

Eventually, the ship traffic and their escorts of trailing gulls all fell astern, and ahead, Dieter soon saw a distinct line; the water was a deeper blue-green.

"Gulf stream?"

Another nod. Again, Charlie lifted the binoculars and surveyed all 360 degrees, then reached for the throttles. He pulled them back almost to idle, then set the auto-pilot so that they made a large circle, still west of the indigo stripe that was the western border of the warm river of the gulf stream. He then motioned for Dieter to follow him down to the deck. It was already getting warm, and they sat in the main cabin, out of the sun, the ice chest between them. Dieter fished for another jar of tea while Charlie reached under the starboard seat cover and extracted a framed piece of slate; a child's toy blackboard, and chalk. Dieter's first thought was historical. It was like the reverse of when Karl Czerny and others wanted to converse with Beethoven! They would write their thoughts and questions down on similar slates or notebooks, the deaf master would read them, then offer his own responses vocally.

The first thing Charlie wrote was, "Any experience with boats?"

Finally, an ice-breaker! Delighted, Dieter happily told him he had. "Until my accident, I belonged to a sailing club on Long Island. We sailed class boats, Solings mainly, and occasionally larger craft. I'm very much at home on the water."

Charlie's burnished face seemed to soften a bit. He smiled for the first time and nodded. Then he wrote, "I think better out here."

"I understand. I know you brought me out here for a reason, Charlie. What is it? Is something wrong? I must have said something last night that upset you, but for the life of me, I can't figure out what it was."

Charlie paused, looking down. Then he took a deep breath, hesitated another moment, and wrote, "You cannot marry Suzi."

Dieter felt like he'd been slapped in the face. A hundred disjointed thoughts bombarded his brain at once, but the only one he could verbalize was, "Suzi and I have been all through the race thing. It's not a problem."

Charlie's frown and rapid shaking of his head told Dieter there was something else. The chalk flew: "Nothing like that."

"What, then? I don't understand."

Again Charlie Everette hesitated before writing. His face showed something between agony and fury. Dieter could tell he was trying hard to keep himself under control.

He wrote, "Susan is my daughter." Which he erased quickly, then wrote, in larger letters, "And you are my son."

The impact of that sentence on Dieter was as if some cruel devil-surgeon had cut out his heart and his tongue in the same instant. He could make no reply, and instantly felt a cold sweat all over his body. Several minutes passed before he could say anything, but then denial and disbelief took hold. "What are you saying? That's crazy. Impossible!"

With that, Charlie laid the blackboard on the deck, got up and walked to the trunk resting on the afterdeck. Dieter was too much in shock to do more than stare while Charlie fished in his pocket for a key, bent to unlock the trunk, and lifted the lid. He removed a number of items of sailor's clothing, and an ugly looking pistol, then extracted something that sent Dieter further into misery.

It was a uniform.

Faded and patched, it was nonetheless intact; a uniform Dieter had seen often as a small child, in several photographs his mother had showed him of a dashing *Kriegsmarine* officer, Knights Cross around his neck.

Speechless, Dieter waited for him to pick up the blackboard again. In perfect *Hochdeutsch*, Charlie scribed, "*Ich bin Korvettenkapitan Horst Johann von Hellenbach. Deine Mutter ist Elisabeth Kroll.*"

He handed Dieter the blackboard and climbed to the flying bridge again. Dieter vaguely understood that he was ostensibly checking on their position and traffic, but was really giving him some time to absorb this incredible revelation. Dieter felt like a fish yanked from its comfortable blue depths, gaffed, and left to die a flopping, gasping death on the sun-drenched deck. Somewhere in the recesses of the part of his mind that was still functioning, he recalled something Suzi had said when we were at the lighthouse museum. "*I've seen Daddy stare at that stuff the same way you are. What's so interesting about it? That was a long time ago. Before we were born...*"

Suzi...Suzi, my love, my— *half sister??*

By rights, Dieter thought he should have felt the complete spectrum of every natural emotion that can be put to words; sorrow, anger, self-pity, rejection, guilt, every negative feeling known to people who love, but all he knew in that moment was a vast emptiness, a void deep as the ocean they floated upon and wide as the horizon stretching before them. He could not go to the Mayo Clinic for this problem, and for once in his life, felt a tinge of regret that he'd never been a religious man, yet doubted if God Himself could have helped just then. He also wondered what the man up on the flying bridge was thinking. Feeling. *Could this man really be my father? Could any of this insanity be true?*

The rest of the morning and most of the afternoon they drifted on the edge of the gulf stream while the man with the iron hair and callused hands wore out piece after piece of chalk: "Sunday's story was true up to a point. . ."

Up to the point that she had rescued and brought back to health a wounded sailor all right, but his ship had been a U-boat, sunk by a Yank Destroyer after having been spotted by a plane. Horst von Hellenbach was the only survivor, blown from his conning tower into the water. His loss of memory had been a convenient lie.

"By the time I recovered, the war was over."

"Why didn't you surrender and go back to Germany?"

"To what? A bomb crater? A trial as a spy? War criminal? Prison?"

"You had a family."

"I didn't *know* I had a son. Besides, with the passage of time, I came to realize that Elisabeth had never loved *me*. She had only been attracted to my titled name, and my "glorious and heroic" military exploits. Social status and fame was what she really wanted."

Dieter had to then tell Charlie what he had already guessed, that Elisabeth had married his brother.

"And lost no time doing it either, I'll wager. Are there other children?"

"No, I'm the only one."

"And I am proud of what you have done with your life."

No comment from Dieter on that.

"You were correct to renounce it all," he wrote. "The name, the era, the terrible history. Every day of my exile was a day of atonement. Of silent repentance for what I had done and what I had been a part of."

"I can believe that. Have you been happy here? With Sunday?"

"What is happiness? Suzi was my happiness. Yes, I do love Sunday, and respect her enormously, like everyone else who knows her. She is the most remarkable human being I have ever known, but Suzi is my own flesh and blood. I adore her more than life itself."

A long lapse of 'conversation' followed. Dieter simply could not think of anything else to say, and it seemed useless to try telling this man that Suzi had also become the light of his own life, and that no one could love her more than he did. The truth was, his head was empty. Empty as the tea-jar he was holding. The only thing more vacuumed was his soul.

Charlie—Dieter still could not bring himself to call him Father—must have sensed his despair. He stood, walked to the aft rail, and motioned for Dieter to join him. He pointed down, then walked back, picked up the blackboard and wrote one final series of his own thoughts:

"Down there, beneath this very spot, are all my shipmates. They died with wartime honor. I live like a shadow with none. But I am proud to have you as my son."

There was mist in his pale blue eyes, and when he offered his hand, Dieter grasped it in both his own, hugged him, then turned away so that Charlie could not see his own tears.

Like a silent travel film being shown backwards, they returned toward the setting sun to the marina. Not another word, glance, or gesture passed between them, then, or on the drive back to Manteo. After the old pickup disappeared, Dieter sat on the porch steps for a long time, trying to pick a path through the maze of his thoughts. The last thing he would remember clearly of the night of that day was wandering all over Roanoke Island on his ten-speed, trying to find Suzi.

He never did.

◆

Chapter 13

The following day, after a restless night, Dieter rode down to Wanchese. As he'd expected, the *BLACK DOLPHIN* was gone. Still, he didn't give up. He went to Suzi's trailer-house, but this time the door was locked. No doubt she was with her parents, then he remembered she had said they sometimes were at sea for weeks at the time. Utterly dejected, he pedaled back to Manteo and went to the Weeping Radish. No one there had seen or heard from her, and the irritated manager told him that if Suzi did not contact him soon, she would lose her job.

He went back home, sat down and tried to get a handle on what to do next. There was nothing he could do to change anything, and there was no way he could concentrate on any work. With nothing left for him on the Island, Dieter decided to leave Manteo. He packed, called a taxi, and before leaving the house, he left his recording of the Tchaikowsky concerto on the table, thinking that if Suzi came back. . .

While waiting for the taxi, which had to come all the way from Nags Head, he made two phone calls.

The first one was to Sy. "Sy, this is Dieter. I'm coming back to New York, but before I do, I'm going to call Dr. Lert and see if he will give me a little of his time."

"You mean you're going to fly out to L.A. first?"

"Yes, if he will see me."

"Dieter, something's wrong. I can hear it in your voice. What's going on?"

"Nothing you won't like to hear. It's over between Suzi and me. I have to get away from here, at least for a while."

"Uh-huh. Well, call me soon as you get to New York."

"I will."

There was no regular air schedule to and from Manteo, but at the tiny airport, Dieter located an independent pilot who was willing to fly him to Raleigh/Durham. While waiting for him to prepare his craft for flight, Dieter walked around the very neat terminal building which was chock full of model planes, photographs, and displays of its history. Apparently, it had been an important link in the shore defenses during the Second World War, with small, privately owned aircraft doing volunteer duty as members of the Civil Air Patrol. Dieter wondered if one of them had been the plane that had spotted his father's submarine.

His thoughts then, and during both the short flight to Raleigh and the long one to Los Angeles, were of a strange, new mixture. He had to adjust his personal psyche to include the fact that he now had a father. Not some vague newspaper clipping-photograph album-paper memory of a long dead Hitler sycophant. Not a small but deadly cog of a grotesque, inhuman war machine blindly doing the bidding of its monster leader. Not a faded sepia image of a man he'd despised as part of the horrible regime he was a willing, believing disciple of, but an actual, living man whom Dieter had found he not only could like and respect, but admire as well. More importantly, he was also a man who, along with his remarkable black queen, had produced the only woman Dieter could ever love. And now, that dead father had returned from his sea-grave and had effectively—and permanently—subtracted the one true happiness from his new life. Dieter hated him more than ever, though he knew he had no reasonable right to.

High above the Rockies, he tried to put those thoughts out of his mind and sleep, but it was not possible. He did, however, finally manage to concentrate on the memory of each precious moment Suzi and he had spent together, thereby temporarily driving the harshness of reality from his aching head and heart.

When the plane landed at LAX, he was dully aware that he had eaten nothing in nearly twenty-four hours. All he'd consumed was coffee, which had no taste. In a sort of non-caring stupor, he ultimately drifted to a hotel room, where he collapsed on the bed, fully clothed, and slept the zombie-sleep of the dead for another twelve hours.

A long, hot bath, a shave, and room-service breakfast restored his physical condition enough to get himself ambulatory again, though his brain still begged to hide behind the false curtain of jet lag. With every ounce of willpower he could summon, Dieter shoved it all back into an unused mental storage closet in the back part of his head, dressed, and went for a long walk. The Los Angeles smog seemed like clean Alaskan air compared to the stinking fog of his emotional state. . .

Dr. Richard Lert let him into his condo, which was located close to the Dorothy Chandler Pavillion. "I am glad to see you, Dieter, but you look like Paganini's death mask. What's the matter?"

"I need to talk to someone. No, not just anyone, I need to talk to you."

"All right," Lert said with a warm smile, "Come, sit down and have a glass of wine. I have found that a glass of really good wine relaxes the blood and frees the tongue at the same time."

The wine glass he handed Dieter was of rare crystal, and while pouring, Lert told him he belonged to an exclusive wine club which met once a month, for the sole purpose of sampling the best vintages money could buy. "I live rather simply, Dieter. I'm too old to indulge in all my past loves, except my scores and an occasional glass of good wine. What brings you here?"

The wine Lert had poured was no doubt better than any Dieter had ever tasted, but he was not in relaxed enough a state to fully appreciate it. Nonetheless, it most certainly did loosen his tongue. Lert poured and Dieter talked-- for nearly two hours. Told him everything; from his student days to the disastrous trip with his resurrected father. When he finally stopped, Lert pulled a chair up directly in front of his own.

"Dieter, do you really and truly want a second career in conducting?"

"Yes, more than anything. My life has to be...worth something."

"Just so. Well, if that is true, then you must rededicate yourself, and I mean totally. You must be able to put everything else aside, out of your head and soul. Do you think you are capable of that much sacrifice?"

"I think so. Yes."

"I am not so sure. You have many dragons to kill. Many demons to exorcise first. But if you are willing, really willing, I will help you all I can. It means you will have to come here, stay with me for a while, and study very, very hard. Can you do that?"

"Yes, sir. I can. When would you like me to start?"

Lert paused for a long moment, his brow knitted into a plowed field. At last, he said, "I can help you with all things musical. It will probably be my greatest accomplishment as a teacher, but I can't work with you when your head is full of stinky cheese. Before we can begin, you must get rid of those demons. I can't help you with that. As a matter of fact, I doubt if anyone can. It is something you have to do alone."

"I understand," Dieter said, feeling all the more miserable. "I only wish I knew where to start."

"I know where to start," Lert replied, standing. He stared down at Dieter for a moment, then turned and left the room. When he came back, he had a pair of scissors in his hand. Dieter was too far out of it to realize what Lert had in mind until he had already cut the glove from the deformed hand. "Honesty," he said, "Is what all your future players will expect from you. And, it is what you must always expect of yourself. This hand is not so terrible to look at. By not hiding it in a closet, it will tell everyone that it is unimportant; that you have no warts to hide, so to speak. Do you follow me?"

Dieter began to see a pinpoint of light at the end of a long tunnel. "Yes. Yes, I do."

"Good. Now, go back to New York, see your agent and be honest with him, too. Then go back to Germany and face down all the demons there. Come back when you can smile and work again. Then we will begin."

He paused again, and said softly. "When my own wife died, I thought I knew what hell was. Thought I could never work again. I was wrong. Suzi will live in a special place deep inside you forever, like a living memory. It will be difficult at first, but you will eventually get beyond your self-pity. There is simply too much of life ahead of you. Too many performances to conduct. Too many people to touch with your talent."

He grinned at Dieter, hugged him like a grandson, and shoved him out the door. On the way back to the hotel, and later going through the airport, Dieter was surprised at how few people glanced at his left hand. . .

Back in New York, Dieter didn't call Sy right away. The first thing he did was grit his teeth and register at the Mayflower, determined to rid himself of that particular psychological demon as well. The staff welcomed him like he might have been the twin brother of the prodigal son, and it did not take him more than a night or two before he slept without bad dreams.

Sy, of course, was delighted to see him, and instantly put his own plan of action in place. Dieter didn't tell Sy the reason for his separation from Suzi. There seemed nothing to be gained by telling him of his new-found father, either. Nor did Dieter tell him immediately that he was planning to go back home for a long overdue visit. For his part, Sy never questioned him about Suzi, for which Dieter was truly grateful. For Sy, it was simply enough that Dieter had "come to his senses" and was ready to get on with his life and career. Yet, Sy was not so insensitive that he was willing to set Dieter adrift in Manhattan with nothing to do, at least not at night. By day, Dieter spent a lot of his time in the library or in his room, reading everything he could get his hands on relating to World War Two history; books by Churchill, Trevor-Roper and Shirer, among others, some of the German historians, Heinrich Boll, Gunther Grass, and many of the 'apologists.'

And, with Sy, there was a light *divertissement* every single night; a play, concert, movie, or ball game. (Sy was a great Knicks fan.) Each evening would invariably wind up at the Deli, where Dieter ate light and Sy ate heavy, talking well into the morning about everything under the sun except music. One night, Sy had forgotten tickets, and they had to drive all the way to his house in Brooklyn Heights to get them. Dieter had not been there since before Sy's third divorce, and was appalled at the way his manager was living. The place was a disaster area. A veritable *Schweinerei!* Dieter held his tongue about it until they sat down at the Deli. Then he pried a little. "Sy, what happened?"

"Pardon?"

"With you and Ruth."

"Oh," he said between bites of corned beef on rye. "Sweat."

"I'm sorry?"

"Sweat. Perspiration. My glands."

"What the devil are you talking about?"

"Look, Ruthie didn't mind my being fat—"

"Portly."

Sy laughed. "Fat! Face it. Anyway, she didn't care about that. 'I like big men,' she always said, and we were terrific in bed. Terrific! But... I sweat. She couldn't take my dripping all over her body every other night. Christ, Dieter, you think you got woman problems? Look at *me*. Three wives and three shrinks and I'm in the market for another one of each."

"You're not serious."

Sy took a quick swipe at his mouth with his napkin and went on, "Oh yes, I am. Listen, first there was Naomi. Robert's mom. Whined all the time about the frantic pace of my life. Our life. Especially after Robert was born. My analyst said, 'Don't give in to her'. I didn't, and she left, taking Robby with her. Then there was Tammy. You remember Tammy, don't you? The one with the boobs? Jesus, did she have a chest!"

Sy took a long swallow of beer. "But she couldn't take my friends. 'They're all too *intelleckchall'*, she says, and my new shrink says, 'Slowly, gently, try to improve her. Take her to the opera, the ballet, concerts, plays.' Hell, Tammy's top cultural level was tag-team wrestling at the Garden! So *I* left. Then I marry Ruth, and my latest guy, Hermann, says, 'Relax. Cut back some.' Relax? Me? So I sweat all over Ruthie's body and *she* leaves."

He pushed his plate away, leaned back, and tried unsuccessfully to mute a belch. "I'll tell you something, Dieter. Life's a bitch. A regular bitch, but somewhere in this town there's a nice Jewish girl who can keep up with me, likes all my *intelleckchall* friends, and sweats like a kosher pig. I'll find her, too."

Dieter found he was laughing so hard he had tears in his eyes, also realizing it was the first time he had done so in quite a while. "Another analyst, too?"

"Sure. I have to have a steady shrink, Dieter. Otherwise, I'd start *thinking* about all this crap and never get any work done."

Dieter's laughing broke out again. "You're a piece of work, Sy. Really good for me. Even when you're lying, you're good for me."

"Yeah? Well, let's get out of here. There's this place downtown I want to show you. . ."

Three days later, Dieter felt in secure enough frame of mind to face down his last demon, and bought a round trip ticket to Frankfurt.

◆

Chapter 14

Inspectors Volker and Schneider knew the routine, having gone through it time after time. Carrying their written reports, they knocked on their boss's door, were admitted and told to take seats. Both men were tired and suffered from lack of sleep, but were well prepared and knew this session would be a short one. Each would give a brief oral summary of their findings, and then leave detailed files for the boss to study.

"Well?" the policeman said. "Who wants to go first?"

Volker was senior, so he volunteered. "I will, Chief." He cleared his throat. "There wasn't much to add to the von Hellenbach file we don't already have. Our low-grade surveillance on the family continues at Freiburg. Nothing new to report from there. I assume your contact in the U.S. is still watching the musician.

"However, there is one curious fact we didn't have before. I was able to obtain a copy of the standard Notification-of-Death letter sent to the families of all of Korvettenkapitan von Hellenbach's crew, notifying them of the loss of their U-Boat in battle. The reason we hadn't dug it out sooner was because it didn't originate from the Naval administration. It came from Reichsleiter Bormann's office."

The policeman nodded. "That fits. I presume the signature was forged?"

"Yes, sir. We are fairly certain of that. However, I had one piece of good luck. One former member of his crew did survive the war and is still alive. We located him through the pension bureau. One Oskar Knapp. It seems he was in a hospital at Trondheim just before the war ended. Had contracted gangrene and lost part of one leg."

"Where is this Knapp fellow now?"

"Living in Hamburg. Works at a waterfront bar as a stockman. Lives alone in a cheap walk-up. As for the rest, we are sure they are all dead, officers and ratings. And, as you already know, von Hellenbach was living with his fiancée at that small cottage on the Baltic when he disappeared. His death notice letter was sent to his mother, who died shortly after the war ended. It was her other son, Harald, who carried the news to Fraulein Kroll, and married her soon afterward."

"Good report, Friedrich. You see, we now know a couple things we didn't know before. Nice work. You may get that leave after all. What about you, Willi? What were you able to find out?"

"Sir," Schneider said, "Neither the British nor the Americans' records show any U-Boat sinking's in the time period we are investigating. Also, every German boat and crew, whether in port or at sea, are accounted for except the one von Hellenbach commanded. All surrendered as they were ordered to, and were taken into custody. There is no record anywhere of von Hellenbach's boat. It is as if it did not exist. Admiralty records show that only two of the new type U-Boats were built at Trondheim, both of which are accounted for.

"Sir, I believe there was a third boat built there, in total secrecy. It's the only logical explanation."

The policeman grinned at his scholarly subordinate. "Willi, in our business, one of the first things we learn is that as soon as two people know about something, it is no longer a secret. Of course there was a third boat, and I am sure she sailed with a valuable cargo. Namely, one Reichsleiter of the Third Reich, and some fifty million in gold which on today's market would be worth five times that much."

He leaned back in his chair. "My compliments to you both. Leave your files on my desk and go back to what you were doing before."

As soon as his assistants were gone, he punched the intercom for his secretary.

"Sir?"

"I will be driving to Hamburg tomorrow. This time I will take the black suitcase. I may be gone for several days."

"Yes, sir. You told me to hold all your calls. Can you now take the one on the black phone? He has been holding for half an hour."

The policeman picked up the black phone. "Yes?"

"This is Johnny. I guess I will be able to take a few days off."

"Why?"

"The subject has just bought a round trip plane ticket to Frankfurt. Looks like he's going home for a while. The ball's in your court."

◆

Chapter 15

Except for his successful European concert tours back in '74 and '76, Dieter had been home for a brief visit only once since his enrollment at Julliard. His mother had never openly chided him for that, nor had his stepfather. Both fully understood the reasons for his self-imposed 'exile', although he was certain they both always felt a deep resentment that he had shortened his name. That he had been a major figure on the International musical stage mollified them to some degree, Dieter supposed. He had never given more than cursory thought to the strange fact that the complimentary German press had never dug into his background enough to discover or publish his tacit protest at being known as the last of the von Hellenbach line.

The name went far back into German military history. Dieters's male ancestors, proud as any Prussian, had fought with distinction in two centuries of war, and Dieter knew that if Germany had won the last one, he would have been expected to become not an 'effete musician', but an officer cadet as his father, grandfather, and great-grandfathers had. He also knew that had history turned out that way, and knowing he was neither suited nor cared for a military life, he would have been expected to do the next most honorable thing and put a pistol to his head. None of this was ever spoken of while Dieter was a post-war boy growing up, naturally, but there had been a plethora of family albums, portraits, and military mementos scattered around his home to remind him of his lineage every day of his life. Mustached, plume-helmeted, stiff-backed ghosts clanked back and forth in every room. By the time he had been eleven or twelve, they, and his country's most recent history, had nearly suffocated him. It had been easy for him to lose himself in music; hiding from those sabre-scarred shades in his own attic room, behind a closed door, filling the tiny space with scales, arpeggios, and basic violin repertoire. When he was accepted at Julliard, it was like he had escaped from prison. Dieter loved his still beautiful mother as much as any son, but as he'd grown older, and enjoyed some success away from home, had found it was quite possible, even preferable, to love her at long distance.

Riding south now in the comfortable first class compartment of the fast *Eilzug* from Frankfurt to Freiburg, he had to admit to a pair of super-ironic thoughts which flitted through his head like the blurred pastoral images flashing past his window; Of Beethoven--the magnificent Beethoven--who so desperately needed to be accepted as an equal by the bill-paying upper crust of early 19th century society, he was willing to falsify his peasant name by adding the prefix of 'noble lineage' to it. Instead of heading south from Bonn to make his musical mark at Vienna simply as Ludwig Beethoven, the poor but defiant son of a drunk and a cook, he—like his hero Napoleon, who had arrogantly added 'Emperor' to his own name—wished to bring the world to his feet as Ludwig *von* Beethoven, though he was shrewd enough to use the Dutch equivalent of 'van'. How the aristocracy must have laughed at him. Yet, his staggering talent eventually overcame the youthful *faux pas,* which he stubbornly clung to all his life.

The second thought Dieter found himself turning over and over in his mind as the wheels beneath him clicked in perfect duple meter, was how many times he had heard his stepfather mutter to no one in particular how Hitler had 'done so many good things' as well as the bad; like how the trains ran on time, and what a wonder of modernity the *Autobahn* was! His stepfather! His father's tall, too-handsome twin brother, whose very name Dieter had despised since puberty. Even as a child, he'd been sure Harald von Hellenbach had considered being de-nazified by the occupying Allies the absolute worst humiliation a man could endure. Dieter had often wondered, therefore, why he had not placed a pistol to his own temple! But then, he had to remember that if Harald had had the courage to perform such an act, he would have done it long ago, when a clubfooted birth defect had prevented him from becoming the brilliant cadet and officer his older twin had. Dieter didn't think his stepfather had ever been satisfied that a respectable career as a surgeon came even remotely close to his father's prestige. *Well, he had gotten my mother as compensation, hadn't he? Where was the justice of that?*

Whether under summer's dark green umbrella or winter's white blanket, the Black Forest region of Germany was, in Dieter's mind at least, the most beautiful in the country. The family home was actually not in Freiburg itself, but some six kilometers west, in Klingendorf, on the far slope of the *Gloettertal*. The large house was typical of the area, built of timbers that would last yet another hundred years, and filled not only with clocks, but stuffed fowl and antlered heads of animals Harald von Hellenbach had, over time, shot in lieu of the enemies of the Fatherland.

Dieter arrived in time for the afternoon ritual of *Kaffee und Kuchen*, was made comfortable in a living room which had not changed in five generations except for the addition of a Blaupunkt color television set with a large screen. He informed his mother and Harald that he was thinking of staying a week or two. In fact, he had no idea how long he'd be there. When he had boarded the train at Frankfurt, he'd had every intention to tell his mother, the first chance he had alone with her, the truth about his real father. But when she hugged him, with tears in her eyes as she tried unsuccessfully to ignore the now uncovered hand, Dieter had second thoughts. The time to tell her about his father would present itself soon enough. Better to wait for the right moment.

She was dressed the same as always; drab sweater-and-skirt combination that had always seemed one style-notch beyond widows' weeds. Her hair was pulled back into the traditional severe bun, and she wore, as usual, a minimum of makeup. Dieter was glad it was winter, because Harald wore a heavy wool suit, thus sparing everyone the sight of ugly legs and knobby knees protruding from the greasy-looking *Lederhosen* his stepfather usually paraded around in like some grotesque, gray-haired member of the Hitler Youth.

Harald stuck around only long enough to hear his story about studying with Dr. Lert. When Dieter mentioned that Lert, the son of a well-to-do Viennese banking family who had married Vicki Baum was his new mentor, he said, “They were Jews!”

Dieter couldn’t resist retorting, “Yes. Among the lucky few who survived.”

As he so often had, Harald mumbled something under his breath and left the room.

“You shouldn’t provoke your father like that, Dieter.”

“He’s not my father, but you’re right, I shouldn’t waste my breath. I’m sorry, Mutti, he always affects me like a splinter under my fingernail, but I suppose I have no right to antagonize him in his own house.”

“That’s true. Besides, he really is your father, at least the only one you ever had. He’s always thought of you as his own son.”

Dieter felt his blood rising, and decided to change the subject. “Well, why don’t you let me treat you to dinner tonight. Is the *Fassanenhaus* still open?”

“Oh, yes. That would be nice. Wonderful idea.”

Truth was, Dieter wanted to go to that well-known mountain *Gasthaus* called “The Pheasant House” anyway. No other restaurant he had ever been in could match the splendid wild game, which was the specialty there, and after eating so much American food, he was anxious to plow into some roast duckling and red cabbage. He also knew Harald and his mother went there often, and would be pleased to have their friends see their famous son show up there with them.

They went, and Dieter was not disappointed.

He had no chance to visit alone with his mother until the following Monday, when Harald went to the hospital for his rounds. Dieter took a morning walk, and when he got back, found her in his study, polishing the furniture.

"It's really cold out there. Let's make some coffee, Mutti."

"All right. I'd like a cup myself."

He waited until they were sitting in the kitchen before asking, "Mutti, may I have a look at your scrapbooks?"

Her eyebrows shot up instantly. "Certainly, but why? You haven't looked at those old pictures since you were a boy."

"I know. Maybe I have finally matured enough, but I really want to see them now. Would you mind?"

She got up without a word, and came back only moments later, beaming. "I was going through these again just last week. You know, you truly were an adorable little fellow."

She placed half a dozen large cardboard-backed albums on the kitchen table, sat down next to Dieter, and poured another cup of her delicious coffee, obviously pleased at his request. Dieter opened the first one, knowing full well she had stacked them in order. It was the very first one he was interested in; the one that included the only photographs of his father. The first few pages were neatly organized with faded holiday snapshots of the three of them; his father, Harald, and the pretty young teen-age girl both of them had been in love with.

Dieter studied the grainy pictures, looking for the resemblance between Horst von Hellenbach and Charlie Everette. He didn't really see it until the fourth page, which showed his father in full uniform, smiling at the professional cameraman. Dieter stared for a full two minutes. There could be no mistake. There, before his unwilling eyes, was a much younger version of Charlie Everette, only with blond hair and no scars. Dieter vaguely remembered his mother's telling him of the occasion. "Where was this taken, Mutti? I forgot."

"Why, it was in a restaurant in Berlin, after your father's medal ceremony. We were both so happy then. We became engaged that night, you know."

"Where are the pictures of the actual ceremony?"

Her face immediately turned crimson. "Well, I... They are in a secret place. I didn't think it was wise to keep them with the others, you know. . ."

"I understand. May I see them?"

"Are you sure you want to?"

"Yes, Mutti, I'm sure."

Five minutes later she returned carrying a handful of photographs, which had long since been removed from any scrapbook guests or relatives might have wished to see. Seven or eight clear pictures of Adolf Hitler presenting the Knights Cross to his father. Hitler beaming at him. Hitler shaking his hand. Goering leading him by the arm toward a number of important guests who crowded the great hall of the *Reichchancellery*. Goebbels shaking hands with grinning members of his father's crew, and bending over his mother's hand like a Baron in a Viennese operetta.

Dieter managed a weak, nauseous smile, but his mother didn't notice. Viewing those pictures again had transported her back in time to a momentous occasion. "Oh, it was grand, Dieter. That night was like a fairy-princess tale for me. I had a new, expensive dress, and wore real jewels. Don't you think I was pretty?"

"You were beautiful," Dieter whispered, putting an arm around her thin shoulders. "What's the date? I can't read it any more."

"November 20, 1944. I shall never forget it. Your father was so proud. So handsome."

"Where was Harald? Wasn't he there, too?"

"Yes. He was there."

Dieter gazed at the pictures again. Something had caught his eye. "Who's this man?" He stuck his finger-tip on the face of a beefy man who had been in several of the photos.

His mother peered down, furrowed her brow, and replied, "That's Oskar. Oskar Knapp. He was with Horst on every cruise. Chief of the Boat, I think he was. Ranking petty officer."

"Look here, Mutti, the same man is in this picture of Father's memorial service. Apparently he didn't go on the last patrol."

"No, he didn't. He went into the hospital for an emergency operation just before Horst—"

"Before Father's last voyage?"

"Yes." Her eyes had clouded. "He stayed in touch for years after the war. A rather crude man as I recall, but quite sincere. He worshiped Horst."

"Is he still alive?"

"He must be. I think he lives in Hamburg. Or did when we heard from him last. Why?"

"I'd like to see him. Talk to him. Did you save his address?"

"I'm sure I have it here somewhere. Let me look."

While she was gone, Dieter quickly leafed through the other albums, hardly giving a glance to the pictures of his mother's wedding to Harald, the silly child-pictures of himself, and the too-painful shots of his first recital. The other albums held no interest for him. He had found what he'd had been looking for, and resolved to say nothing of the Everette family to his mother or to Harald until he had a chance to talk to Oskar Knapp, if he could find him.

◆

Chapter 16

Dieter didn't think it was possible to be colder anywhere else in the world than at the sprawling Hansa metropolis of Hamburg in the dead of winter. It had been his bad luck to experience that part of the year each time he'd gone there. With an east wind blowing, the wet-cold assaulted the body like a million stabs of icicle daggers, and no amount of clothing or the rum-and-tea mix they called grog was enough protection against it, especially on the waterfront, nor did the temperature freeze the smells. The inner city, with its impressive buildings, the two pretty *Alster* lakes, expensive restaurants and hotels, was like a separate city altogether from the edge of the filthy Elbe, only a few kilometers away.

And it was in the waterfront district he found Oskar Knapp.

Working as a stockman in one of the smelly sailors' bars.

In spite of his age, Knapp had added many solid pounds to an already enormous bulk, and with his shaven head and a face that looked like murder about to happen, he looked, and Dieter was sure that given the right occasion, could act such a role admirably. Yet, Oskar

Knapp, Dieter was to discover, was a veritable marshmallow inside. When Dieter found him and introduced himself, Knapp shed real tears, and begged Dieter to come back around when his shift ended.

Knapp took Dieter to his apartment, which was no more than a cold water flat in a nearby building as filthy as the alley in front of it. Dieter was therefore surprised that the two third-floor rooms were clean and neat as any medical clinic. Knapp noticed his appreciative smile. "Old military habits die hard, son. So. You're my *Herr Kaleun's* kid? Be damned. I didn't even know he had one. Hey, sit down and tell me all about yourself. Can I offer you a Schnapps? Only thing I know can take the chill out of your bones this time of year."

"Thanks. I could use one. It's nasty out there."

One was enough. The liquor tasted faintly of peppermint, and set Dieter's throat and belly on fire, but inside a minute, had warmed his toes and the fingertips of his good hand. Inside the next thirty minutes, Dieter had removed his overcoat and scarf, and was telling his father's old chief a highly condensed version of his life story up to the time of the Central Park shooting. It never occurred to him whether or not the burly but amiable former submariner might look down his nose at him—the son of a war hero, but one who played the violin and had renounced everything his family had stood for.

Knapp listened politely, and then commented, "I'm sorry about your hand, but I'll bet you'll be a fine conductor. Your father would have been proud of you. This I know."

"You knew him well, didn't you?"

"As much as anyone, I imagine. You serve with somebody like him for nearly five years in quarters close as ours, and through forty hells, you get to know a man inside out. I loved him, son. We all did."

"Will you tell me about him? About your war and all?"

Knapp dropped his head. Seemed to be studying the tops of his shoes. Dieter could have sworn there was fresh moisture in his eyes. Without looking up, Knapp said, "I will if you'll take me to The Alster Pavillion tomorrow."

"I'll be glad to take you anywhere you wish to go. Why the Alster Pavillion?"

The gentle giant raised his head. "When he left me in that Norwegian hospital before my operation, your father's last words to me were, 'When all this madness is over, Chief, I'll treat you to dinner at the finest restaurant in what is left of our Fatherland.' He never got the chance, and I never got my treat, which would have been, for me at least, far better a reward than any stupid medal the Third Reich could have dreamed up. So, it would be nice to go to Hamburg's finest spot and toast his memory in the company of his only son. I'm sentimental that way, I guess. Come to think of it, you're just as tall, and you look a little like he did. On second glance though, you favor your mother more. She was a great beauty. Anyway, what about it? Will you buy this old sailor a meal in a fancy-shmanzy restaurant? I hear they have a little orchestra there, and the best beer in West Germany. I'll even wear a coat and tie."

"It's a deal, Chief Knapp. The Alster Pavillion it is. Shall I pick you up?"

"Not necessary. At today's prices, a taxi would cost you more than the meal. I'll take the *Strassenbahn* and meet you there at five. And call me Oskar, please."

"Fine, Oskar. But why so early?"

Knapp grinned. "Because eating a meal like that is like being in bed with a pretty woman. One needs to take his time. Besides, it may take until they close up for me to tell you about your father. . ."

". . . And when he got his first command, he insisted on two things: A good Chief Engineer for the boat and a good cook for the men. Speaking of cooks, I wish old Kirchner could be here with us. He'd appreciate this rumpsteak."

The beef was good, Dieter agreed, along with everything else they ate and drank. With mutes on, the tiny stringed "orchestra" playing Johann Strauss and other composers of *Unterhaltungsmusik* so softly as to be nearly inaudible, the entire atmosphere of the evening was turning into a most enjoyable – and enlightening – experience. "You called him 'Herr Kaleun.' I don't know that word," Dieter said.

"That was what U-Boat crews called commanders they respected and liked. Talk about respect, there wasn't a man among us who wouldn't have followed your father right into Hades. Matter of fact, there were times when he took us there! At least that's what we thought, but he brought us out every time. At sea, everything depended on the good judgment of the commander; our success in battle, and our very lives. It was awesome responsibility."

Oskar drank deeply, smacking his lips with genuine

pleasure. "God, this is good beer. I'll tell you something else about leadership, son. You may know that in spite of losing six out of every ten men in the submarine service, we were faithful and committed right up to the end. But it wasn't because of any loyalty or affection for that insane little Austrian corporal. Most Kriegsmariners hated him. It was for our commanders. Men like your father, and Uncle Karl."

"Uncle Karl?"

"Admiral Doenitz."

"Oh."

"Wasn't much shit, pardon the language, we went through that he hadn't also gone through in the first war. That's probably why he looked the other way when your father bent the rules now and then."

"What rules?"

"Those that saved our stinking lives. Like, whatever boat we were in, he'd take her straight down a hundred feet past her rated depth without batting an eye. First time he did that, we all nearly died from fear that the sea pressure would crush us, but it didn't, and the ash cans the Allies dumped on top of us didn't kill us either. There were other maneuvers he'd do that weren't by the book. Lots of them. I'll give you one example: One time we found ourselves smack in the middle of a large convoy heading to Russia. Pretty stormy weather, which we loved. Just before dawn, we spent every single torpedo we had on board. I don't know how many ships we sent to the bottom that night. Herr Kaleun knew boats and lives were lost by ego-crazy commanders who liked to poke their periscopes up to watch and confirm kills, using up precious escape time.

Your father had not shot at the fattest, slowest target, either. He simply took us underneath that slow freighter like an egg under a hen, and used her for cover. We stayed under her keel until midnight of the next day, and then got clean away. Pulled the same trick once in the Med, too. You know what his nickname was?"

"What?"

"The Wizard. There wasn't any dozen English or American Captains who could either catch him or kill him. Listen, the enemy was reading our codes faster than we were by then. Knew exactly where we were and how many of us were out there. Still, the Wizard outfoxed them. Oh, he had seafaring magic in his head, that's for sure. By far the best of all of them. You know about our aces, don't you?"

"Well, I've done a little reading."

"There were several. Prien was the first."

"The hero of Scapa Flow."

"Right. He, Kretschmer, and Schepke were like the three musketeers. Your dad was a bit like all of them. I mean, he had Prien's determination, Kretchmer's quiet style, and Schepke's guts. But he had more brains than all of them put together."

"Those other three died, didn't they."

"Right again. All three at practically the same time on the same patrol. But that bastard Hitler kept Admiral Doenitz from telling anybody until long after the fact. Uncle Karl lost two sons, too. One in a U-Boat. They say when Doenitz heard the news, he never even twitched. If that mad son of a bitch Hitler had listened to him, things might have turned out different. The civilized world should thank God he didn't. But serving in those boats was no picnic."

Dieter lost any appetite he might have had for dessert, listening to Oskar describe the appalling conditions he and his mates lived in while on long patrols. Life on a submarine, according to him, was just the opposite of the glamorous, swashbuckling adventure the Nazi propaganda touted. "Try to imagine being cooped up in a narrow piece of sewer pipe with fifty other guys, one toilet, no way to wash clothes or dry them. Hell, our underwear was even died black. 'Whore's undies' we called them. The stench of rotting food and body odor was so bad you were glad of any excuse to go on deck, no matter what might be up there; planes, destroyers, blizzards, or whatever. I tell you, rats lived better on a garbage scow, even after we got the snorkels. Plus, there was the constant terror of being bombed, shelled, rammed, or depth-charged. By the time the war ended, we'd lost over half the boats we built."

"But the Wizard brought you through everything."

"That he did, and we scored plenty, too. From the beginning, the "happy times" as we called those early years when the pickings were good, before the enemy perfected their radar and the *Amis* came into the war with their millions of planes and ships, and through all the shit we found ourselves in later. Right though it all. Through the misery of knowing, absolutely *knowing* our next patrol was going to be our last. We lost a lot of good mates those last two years, son. Those of us who survived got pretty little pieces of ribbon."

"My mother showed me the pictures of your medal awards ceremony, and the party afterwards."

Oskar, having finally had enough to eat, wiped his mouth, belched into it, then leaned back and laughed. "*Ach*, what a farce. Another piece of Goebbel's pure propaganda. By then, Hitler desperately needed to show off a few heroes who were still alive! Your father was the leading ace at the time, so he was chosen. Got the Knight's Cross with diamonds. All the rest of us got the Iron Cross First Class, but what we liked most was the bath beforehand and the booze after. I was drunk for three days in a row!"

Dieter hadn't noticed that the musicians had packed up and left. Oskar fell silent while the waiter cleared their table and brought brandy, glasses, and cigars.

"That was some weekend, all right. Never forget it." Oskar took his time lighting the cigar, glancing askew at Dieter, who had left his on the table. Oskar rolled it around between his thick lips, puffed a few times, and went on, "Next day, Doenitz made a surprising decision. Not wanting to attend a medal ceremony one week, and then have to go to a memorial service for the same guys the next, he decided not to send your father or me back to sea. After a month touring the country for Goebbels' propaganda machine— on Hitler's orders, by the way, your father and I were assigned to the Grand Admiral's staff, and given cushy training jobs. For a couple months, we thought the war was over for us. Fat chance."

"What happened?"

"What do you think? Things got so bad he had to send us all out again. Even Commander Schnee--his right arm at staff--had to go back out, albeit in one of the new 'dream' boats."

Oskar's eyes misted again as he described the giant type XXI submarine Doenitz had constantly begged Hitler for, but by the time they had been built and ready for use, it was far too late in the war for any but desperate patrols. "She was some machine, Dieter. Twice as big as our old type VIIC, streamlined like Marlene Dietrich, with living quarters that seemed to us like a luxury hotel. She had sophisticated technology for underwater fighting that wasn't improved upon until the Yanks got their nuclear subs. Even had a huge deep freezer! But of more than 90 of them built right here in Hamburg, we only managed to get three of them up to Trondheim. Schnee got the U-2511, Captain Mohr got the U-2512, and your father got one that hadn't even been numbered yet. But there was something terribly wrong about that boat, son. Something—"

"Excuse me sir, we are closing." The waiter interrupted Oskar, politely asking them to pay up. They had lost all track of time! Though Dieter hadn't realized it, Oskar, with glass after glass of the brandy, had been getting steadily drunk, and Dieter wasn't feeling much pain either. Yet he was still clear-headed enough to ask the waiter to call a taxi, and vaguely remembered dropping more than two hundred *Deutschmarks* on the table when they left. He would also remember working like hell, with the assistance of a surly driver, hauling his heavy new friend up three flights of stairs and into his bedroom while the taxi waited outside, motor and meter running. By the time Dieter reached his own hotel, and after a tip he thought more than adequate, he was another hundred D-Marks poorer.

◆

Chapter 17

Dieter was impatient to go back the following day to the "Shark's Tooth", the waterfront bar where Oskar worked, primarily because of a remark the old chief had made and which had stuck in his mind; that there had been something "funny" about the boat which had been his father's last submarine command. By mid-afternoon, when he got out of the taxi, it was sleeting.

The bar was already crowded with noisy, but well-behaved drinkers who collectively were producing a layer of stale blue smoke so thick Dieter couldn't see the ceiling. A barmaid with no eyebrows, dyed red hair, and an enormous bosom took his order for grog, and told him Oskar was sitting in the booth at the rear, apparently waiting for him. Dieter paid for his drink and wove his way through a rough looking crowd who paid him not the slightest bit of attention.

"Ah, here you are," Oskar said, smiling broadly. "I see Elke has given you some anti-freeze. Good. Sit, sit. This is the quietest spot in the joint."

Dieter noticed Oskar was drinking only coffee. He wasted no time getting to the point. "Oskar, last night you mentioned something about your new boat, the unmarked one. What was wrong with it?"

Oskar's smile was quickly replaced by a frown. "Everything. First off, well, let me back up a little. I told you we were assigned to training duty after that bash in Berlin. All of a sudden, your father disappeared for several days, and I didn't see him again until I found myself with new orders and immediate transport--by airplane no less--to Norway! It turned out your father's leave time had been cut short, and he had been ordered to go out one more time. He had insisted on having any of his old crew, with the exception of the men who were married. That was a waste of Uncle Karl's generosity and your dad's consideration, since most of the men didn't have much family left. Their boat was the only place they called home any more. Me, I had never been crazy enough to get married, but I felt sorry as hell for those guys who had lost wives and kids in the bombings.

"Anyway, I got to Trondheim, and took my first look at the new boat. At first I was tickled to death to have such a monster to baby, but it didn't take me long to figure out something was stinko about her, and our mission."

Whether to over-dramatize his tale or he had spoken all this too fast, Oskar abruptly stopped talking, took a few slugs of the coffee, looking around as if to see if others were listening. Then he leaned forward and lowered his voice. "She had no deck guns."

"No deck guns? I don't understand," Dieter said.

"I didn't either! There was no deck gun, either forward or aft. And no machine gun in the conning tower. At first glance, I thought they simply hadn't been mounted yet, but when I looked closer, I immediately saw that instead of gun mounts, there were boat davits built into her decks. Big ones, too."

Dieter didn't know how to respond to this information, and merely lifted his shoulders and eyebrows in question.

Oskar's whisper was incredulous. "Boat davits on a U-boat? That's like a whore in a wedding dress. But that wasn't the worst of it. When your dad and I went aboard, we found the torpedo rooms locked up tight. That's when I looked at your father just like you're looking at me now. 'Don't ask, Chief, not now,' he said. I kept my mouth shut from then on, too, because the pen was crawling with non-Navy personnel. SS men, all over the place, loading the boat with boxes of God only knows what. Those goons and their machine guns scared me shitless, I don't mind telling you. But the absolute worst was when we looked in the galley, and found not one but *two* freezers there, and they were full of meat, all right, only it wasn't the kind you eat, not unless you were a cannibal."

"What? Are you saying those lockers were—"

"Stuffed with dead men. Corpses. Frozen like so many trout and wearing Kriegsmarine uniforms. Two of them were officers!"

"But why?"

"Escape bait, we were told. In case we were attacked. I've thought about it every day and night since then. That was when your father found out I'd hurt my foot, and he took me to the hospital. If he knew why all that weird shit was happening, he didn't mention a word to me. I never saw him again."

Oskar sat silent for a long moment, and rubbed his eyes. "I still can't believe they sunk him after all. So many... So many good men. For years I felt guilty as hell I didn't die alongside him and the others."

Before thinking twice, Dieter also leaned forward, whispering, "They didn't kill him, Oskar. He's still alive."

For a while, what Dieter had said seemed not to register in Oskar's mind. His face remained a big blank. Then, his eyes focused. Narrowed. "What did you say?"

Dieter held his gaze, unblinking. "My father is not dead. He's very much alive and in relatively good health."

Oskar Knapp's face underwent a radical change. Sweat broke out on his forehead. His lips began to quiver. Red started from his collar and moved rapidly upwards. Suddenly he lunged across the table and grabbed Dieter by his coat lapels, his livid face only an inch from Dieter's. "I like a good joke much as the next man, sonny boy, but not one like—Wait a minute. You're telling me the truth, ain't you?"

"Yes. It's true, Oskar."

"Where? Where is he?"

"I can't tell you that."

"Why the fuck not?"

"Because he's still in hiding."

Oskar stared at Dieter for a few moments, and then shook his head as if to clear it of contradictory facts. Dieter could sense he was trying hard to deal with one that had suddenly replaced what he had believed for so many years. Then, a new thought occurred to him. "What about the others? The crew?"

Dieter didn't know what kept him from telling

Knapp everything. Oskar Knapp had been his father's *friend*, as well as his trusted mate, yet some kind of warning signal had gone off in Dieter's brain, though he had no idea why, so he meekly responded, "I don't know."

Again Oskar's eyes narrowed. "You're lying."

Dieter felt his own face turning red, instantly knowing he should not have told Knapp his former Commander was alive and well. And now he had been caught out. Oskar gave him no chance to redeem myself. He stood, leaned over, placing both palms on the table, and said, "I've got things to do. Elke has been more than generous anyway. Listen, you come back day after tomorrow. Same time." Now he sounded like a Chief Petty Officer giving a lowly rating a direct order.

"Why?" Dieter managed.

"Somebody I want you to meet."

With those words, he left Dieter sitting there, and disappeared into a back room. Within two more minutes, Dieter began to feel uncomfortably conspicuous, so he hastily threw on his scarf and coat, and left. It took him another five minutes walking through the freezing rain before he was able to hail a taxi.

Except for unenthusiastic meals, Dieter spent the entire day and a half in his hotel room, trying to make some sense of what he'd learned and trying hard to figure out some way to get back on Oskar Knapp's good side. Why had he not told him part or all of Charlie Everette's story? Why hadn't he told Oskar the skeletons of his mates lay in a rusted iron coffin just off Diamond Shoals in the Graveyard of the Atlantic? The man had every right to know. Who was this person he wanted Dieter to meet?

And, why had Dieter not yet told his mother the truth about her first fiancée? He felt something like a traitor. A coward, only without any inkling why.

He did call his mother to tell her he had found Oskar and would stay in Hamburg a few more days. He tried to take naps. Lackadaisically read the newspaper, noting that Wolfgang Sawallisch was conducting the *Philharmoniker* in an all-Mozart program that night, and he knew it was not the weather that kept him from going. Time dragged by until the hour finally came for him to go back to The Shark's Tooth. He walked out of the hotel into a nice surprise:

Once in a great while, a quick, totally unforeseen winter weather change happens in north Germany. The wind goes southerly, the sun comes out like a lost orphan found, and the change in temperature is so drastic, one is lulled into thinking it is early spring. This unexpected treat was like a tonic. By the time he walked through the double doors of the bar, Dieter was in a much better mood.

Inside, he could see no change. It looked as if the crowd he'd had seen there before had never left. Oskar was waiting in the same booth. "I apologize for acting like a dunce yesterday, son. Let me buy you a drink."

"No problem, Oskar. Thanks, I'll just have a beer."

The former engineer heaved himself up and made his way to the bar. When he returned, a brimming mug in each hand, he was accompanied by a much shorter man, wearing glasses and a natty hat, carrying an overcoat over his arm. Oskar set the two mugs on the table and made the introductions. "Dieter, this is the fellow I wanted you to meet. Herr Rudi Winter, this is Herr Dieter von

Hellenbach. Excuse me for a few minutes, please. Elke needs me to move some boxes."

Watching Oskar walk to the back room again, Dieter stood and shook the proffered hand, which was soft as a woman's "May I join you?" the stranger asked. Dieter could hear no particular dialect in his voice, which was a medium-pitched baritone. "Of course."

The man sat down across from Dieter, where Oskar had been, folding his coat neatly on the bench beside him. He removed his hat and placed it on top of the coat, revealing thinning, dark hair. His complexion was close to swarthy, but fresh-shaven, with deep-set, small blue eyes behind the plain glasses. This was the face of an accountant, or a banker, not some waterfront drifter, and certainly not a sailor of Oskar's vintage. Winter looked to be about Dieter's own age. Dieter's first impression of the man was—Ordinary. Average. Mr. Anyman. Nothing about him stood out in any way. He was wearing an off the rack suit, and a blue button-down shirt with a conservative plaid tie. Very neat, but very nondescript.

His next words shook Dieter to his core. "I am truly sorry about your misfortune last year. A few years ago, I heard you play at the *Liederhalle* in Stuttgart, and have collected most of your recordings. The music world has lost a great talent."

"I hope not forever," Dieter said, "but thank you. What can I do for you?"

He had immediately relaxed, thinking that old Oskar Knapp had adroitly arranged an autograph session with a favor-owed friend or had set him up for an interview with a Hamburg journalist. He was completely bowled over when the stranger said, "After so many years, you have found your father. I want you to help me find mine."

"I beg your pardon?"

"Excuse my bluntness, Herr Bach. Oh, yes, I know that is what you wish to be called. Actually, I know nearly everything about you. Your life and career, your unfortunate shooting in New York, except I lost track of you after that. More to the point, I know a great deal about your father. Far more than you do. You see, I—"

"Listen, you two..." The interruption came, not from Oskar, but from his boss lady, the formidable Elke-the-Red, as he'd called her. "No offense, mind you, but I want you to take whatever business you're talkin' about elsewhere. Beer's on me. Just get out of here. Notice I'm sayin' please."

"But why?" Dieter wanted to know. "We haven't done anything."

"*You* haven't," she gave him an eye-rolling look that said, "*And you ain't gonna, sonny.*" She frowned at his booth companion and leaned over the table. "You, too, copper. You got policeman written all over you. I don't need the likes of you in my place unless it's something official. Bad for business either way. Just don't give me no arguments, take your hats and coats and scat. Like I said, the beer's on me."

Oskar was nowhere in sight. Winter, without a word, got up, put his hat on, and touched Dieter's elbow. "We'd best leave. Come, I know a good place where we can have dinner together."

Once out on the street, Winter pointed north. "The Reeperbahn's only a few blocks away. Let's walk."

Confusion had overtaken Dieter's shock. "Are you really a policeman?" was the first thing he could think of to say.

"I'm afraid I am. That old whore has good eyes." He chuckled, and then stopped. He looked at Dieter sharply and said, "We have to talk, Herr von Hellenbach. You have no idea of how much you and I have in common."

"We do? What, for instance?"

Winter took his arm again, and started walking, as though they'd been bosom buddies for twenty years. "Well, for starters, I happen to know that your father and my father left Trondheim, Norway together in an unregistered U-Boat, and took with them over fifty million dollars worth of stolen Nazi gold."

◆

Chapter 18

Auf der Reeperbahn
nachts, um halb eins...

Dieter found himself remembering the tune and words of the ever-popular old German song. Every major city in the world has its "red light" district. In Hamburg, there is the St. Pauli area, the throbbing heart of which is the Reeperbahn, where, as the song says, almost anything goes. Rudi Winter led him to an intimate but crowded restaurant *cum* nightclub called "Door to Paradise", which was surely 'On the Reeperbahn', and it was at least 'nights, half past midnight.'

When their overcooked dinner was finished and the underdressed female floor show had ended, their actual conversation began. "Interesting locale, isn't it?" Winter said.

"Very," Dieter answered, keeping his tone neutral. "Have you been here before?"

"A few times. For business, however, not for pleasure."

"And what about tonight? Business or pleasure?"

"Some of both. To be truthful, I have been looking forward to making your acquaintance for quite a long time.

I really am an admirer of yours, you know, and I meant what I said earlier about your playing."

Dieter had no reason to doubt his sincerity, but was also certain that the dinner, the wine, and the compliments were all part of a suave tactic to allay his uneasiness. To break down his possible suspicion of a stranger. Except for his brief, half conscious interview with the two New York detectives, he had no knowledge whatsoever regarding police methods, and could not for the life of him help feeling apprehensive. "You said you knew all about me. Why? Am I under some kind of investigation?"

Winter laughed. "No, no. Nothing like that, not officially at least, but you have been an important part of an ongoing private investigation I have been working on my own for many years. As I mentioned, I need help to find my own father, and you are the key. Are you willing to help me?"

"How? And how did you know my father was alive?"

"Good old Oskar told me."

"Oskar!"

"Yes. You know, in the real world, unfortunately, there are far more followers of Judas than Jesus. One only needs to know where to drop the proverbial thirty pieces of silver."

Dieter's instantaneous disgust with Oskar Knapp lasted only a second or two. "You're making me feel as uncomfortable as I am confused. I think you had better explain."

"Gladly, but not here, Herr Bach. Come, let's walk a while. It's still relatively warm outside."

It was *not* warm outside, which did nothing for either Dieter's digestion or his confusion. He was about to ask why they couldn't have finished this strange conversation inside when Winter supplied the answer of his own volition. "One practical habit policemen learn and develop early is never to talk of important things in a close, private place. Much better to be in large crowds. Public places. Out of doors is best."

"You sound more like a spy than a policeman," Dieter said.

Winter laughed again. "Do I? Well, that I will take for a compliment."

Dieter decided enough was enough. All evening long Winter had led him through a polite dance, but had told him nothing at all about himself or who his own father was. Dieter had never heard his mother or Harald mention the name Winter, either in connection to his father or anyone else. Nor had he run across the name in any of his recent historical reading. The name meant nothing to him. And, it was getting colder. He stopped in mid stride, turned to face the mystery man, and asked, "Who is your father, Herr Winter? Earlier you told me some craziness about him and my father sailing away with a lot of Nazi gold. What is this all about?"

"Try to be a little patient, please. Allow me to begin by telling you a few facts." He began walking again, and Dieter had no choice but to keep up while he talked.

For the next several blocks, each step they took side by side was like a step back in Dieter's life. The man knew everything about him, from his birth in the Freiburg Hospital to his visits to Mayo's after he'd been shot. And, in considerable detail. He knew who Dieter's teachers were. Remembered important places he had played. Knew of his long association with Sy, and even knew the names of women Dieter had been with that he himself had forgotten.

"...Oh, yes. I have quite a dossier on you, Herr Dieter Ernst von Hellenbach, and one equally as thick on your father, Korvettenkapitan Horst Johann von Hellenbach, last seen alive at Trondheim, Norway."

"But *why?*"

This time, Winter stopped walking. Both of them were unmindful of the hordes of people going around them, in both directions. On the Reeperbahn, there is no night and day, only light and dark, and in wintertime, mostly dark. As Winter spoke, Dieter became aware they were standing directly in front of a coffee stand, and its aroma hit his nostrils at the same time Winter's astonishing words hit his eardrums. "Because I'd like to get my hands on fifty millions in gold bullion-- which would be worth infinitely more now. Plus, I might also finally locate the father I never knew, and let the son of a bitch know he has a son just as calculating and ruthless as he was. Like I said, you are the key. Once I knew your father was alive, I knew he could lead me to mine."

"So, who exactly *is* your father?"

The garish multicolored neon lights of the coffee stand flashed across the policeman's face, showing a purple-orange distorted grin. "Not a respected war hero type like your father, my friend. In fact, he was one of the most hated men in the Third Reich. Certainly one of the most feared. I am the illegitimate son of Martin Bormann."

In the next moment, before the shock waves of surprise attacked Dieter's knees, he felt Winter's hand grasp his elbow. As he led Dieter to one of the high backed stools in the coffee shop, Dieter had the sudden thought that Winter had carefully planned and executed their walk from the restaurant, timing his revelation perfectly with their arrival at the now empty coffee shop. As if to confirm what Dieter was thinking, Winter said, "The owner of this joint is Greek. Speaks but little German and no English. We can talk further here while we warm up some."

He then signaled the bearded proprietor for two cups, and when they were delivered, Winter reached into an inside pocket of his overcoat and produced a silver flask. "A little Cognac will sweeten this mud a bit, don't you think?"

Dieter had never tasted anything better than that brandy-laced cup of Greek coffee. It also gave him time to absorb what Winter had said, but was at his wits end as how to respond, so he simply sat there, by turn sipping and staring into the paper cup. Only after they were half way through a second medicated cup could he find any words of response. "I thought Bormann died trying to escape from the Reichchancellery bunker after Hitler and Eva Braun committed suicide."

Winter's voice was low. Soft. "Many people believe that, and there are reasons why they do, but no, Martin Bormann left Europe on a U-Boat with your father. This I know, and now, you are only the third person still alive who knows it, not counting your father, of course."

"Who else knows?"

"My mother."

While a part of Dieter's brain was struggling to absorb that statement, another part wondered if he wasn't dealing with an insane person. Dieter was not even sure Winter was a real policeman, let alone whose son he claimed to be. Dieter was beginning to feel backed into a corner he might not be able to escape from, and lashed out. "How do I know you are telling me the truth? You claim to be a policeman, but you haven't even showed me any identification. For all I know, you may be some kind of—"

"Ah, yes. You are asking for my *bona fides*. Very well." From his wallet, Winter removed a laminated, official looking I.D. card with his photograph. It was from the State of Hesse Prosecutor's Department, and identified him as a Chief Inspector for the office of *Amt "D"*.

Dieter studied the card closely and handed it back. "What is Amt D?"

Winter said, "The bureau that tracks down war criminals. Do you know anything of the Nuremberg trials?"

"I've read about them."

"Then you must know that only a couple dozen top Nazis went to trial, and only a handful were actually executed by the Allies. Many were given lesser sentences, and most of those were eventually reduced. We latter-day Germans are a lenient bunch concerning the murderers of the Third Reich. Beyond that, there are well over two hundred known butchers who have never been brought to justice. My father heads the list. Number one. Sentenced to death *in absentia*. Amt "D" is charged with the responsibility, at least on paper, to find and prosecute them. So far, we have been pretty much unsuccessful."

"And your job is to track down your own father?"

"Remember, please, that only three people know he is. My official job is to track down Martin Bormann, convicted Nazi war criminal. I've been working on his case half my life, and naturally, I am not the only one. Apart from old Weisenthal and his Jewish bloodhounds, intelligence agencies of practically every winning country that fought in World War Two have been trying to chase him down. There is now a consensus among professionals involved that he is living well in South America, along with any number of his escaped colleagues, but I happen to know they have tracked the wrong man."

Those words only bewildered Dieter further. He motioned to the droop-eyed Greek for another cup of his strong brew, held it out to Winter for another dollop of his Cognac, took another sip and said, "I don't understand, if you knew Bormann was on board my father's U-boat, why go to all that trouble
to--"

"Excuse me, Herr Bach, but you must realize I only discovered that fact recently, after years and years of tracing records in every place imaginable. During my frustrating trip down one of those blind alleys, I discovered that Oskar Knapp had been a member of your father's crew, the only one who was left behind. And it was Knapp who confirmed my suspicions about how Bormann got himself and the gold out of Germany. He told me much the same story he told you; the strange boat, the SS guards, the secrecy, and so on, which fit nicely with other information I already had. I paid Oskar well to let me know if anyone who was on board that unregistered U-Boat ever contacted him. I was no further along with any of it until you showed up, telling him von Hellenbach was still alive. Are you ready to resume our walk?"

Dieter looked at his watch. It was nearly four in the morning, and he suddenly realized how tired he was. Yet, something put him on guard. He didn't want to allow fatigue to contribute toward any kind of agreement with this man. There was no way on earth he would put his father in the kind of trouble that might result.

Winter must have sensed something of what he was thinking and feeling. They had not walked half a block before he said, "I am a very good policeman, Herr Bach, but I am also a practical man. I know what I am asking of you is a lot. Therefore, I am prepared to offer you something just as valuable in return. *Quid pro quo.*"

"What? Money? I don't need any—"

"Not money. Something more valuable to you, although I'd be willing to bet you wouldn't mind a generous share of that enormous pot of gold. No, I have knowledge of certain facts that could change your life completely, and for the better. Believe me, it would be worthwhile to cooperate with me."

"What facts?"

"Not so fast, Mr. Conductor-to-be. First, do you agree to help me? Where is your father?"

They had come to the walled-off entrance to *Freiheitstrasse*, the infamous street where legalized prostitutes of every nationality, size, color, and persuasion sit behind their glass cubicles like ticket salesgirls at a movie house, negotiating services and prices with any who are interested. Even at this time of night-day, the walled-in street itself was jammed with potential customers and the curious tourists who flock there every night to watch the blatant bartering of flesh, as they say, up close and personal!

They joined the crowd and sauntered through the block-long avenue, not speaking. Again, Dieter had the distinct feeling that Winter had patiently orchestrated their stroll through the Reeperbahn with the skill of Berlioz or Rimski Korsakov, fully expecting him to give in to his request in the end. But he had underestimated his man.

"What if I refuse to cooperate?"

"You won't refuse."

"How can you be so sure?"

"Because you have much to gain, as do I. Besides, if you don't help me, I will be forced to kill you. Ah, look. There's a taxi. Perhaps it's time to go to your hotel.

"What did you say?" Dieter was beginning to feel quite woozy, and was not sure he'd heard accurately.

"You heard me. I don't intend to let you out of my sight until we have a deal. Don't worry, this is not your day to die."

In a state of numb exhaustion, Dieter climbed into the back seat of the taxi, Winter right behind him. He felt his arms, legs and feet slowly going to sleep. He felt no more control over his muscles. Worse, his brain was also beginning to cloud over, like a boat sailing into a fog bank. His last, strained memory of the night was hearing the driver humming the last few measures of the Reeperbahn tune.

Wer nach niemals in Lauschiger Nacht
Einen Reeperbahnbum mel gemacht
ist ein armer Wicht, denn er kennt dich nicht

mein St. Pauli, St. Pauli bei nacht.

◆

Chapter 19

"St. Pauli, my St. Pauli"... Suzi is a naked monster, sitting behind a glass booth. I am running to her but my feet are buried in the sand. I am bogged down. Can't move. Why am I wearing an overcoat and scarf on the Pea Island beach? Wait, there is no sandy beach on the Freiheitstrasse... Someone is laughing at me. Who? Sunday? Sunday's head on Sy Glazer's body. How ugly...Someone else is holding me down with incredibly strong arms. Charlie? What are you doing here, Father? Don't you know you are in danger? Suzi, get out of that booth. You look foolish. Come go swimming with me. The sand is hard against my cheek. Rough as Charlie's hands. Sandpaper... Run, Charlie. Get off me and run, Father, the Gestapo is closing in on you. There! There he is. Martin Bormann is chasing you, Father. Damn you, Sunday, stop laughing at me! The Mayflower. Must get to the Mayflower. But the Mayflower is in New York, not Hamburg. The Frederik the Great is in Hamburg. Old world comfortable, built out of solid gold. Nazi gold, stolen from Jews... Where did you go, Suzi? Help me, Sy, stop eating and get this man off of me. Please. Auf der Reeperbahn, nachts, um halb eins... What time is it? Half

past twelve? "ob du 'n Maedel hast, oder hast keins..." Yes, I had a girl, but lost her... Oh, my God, what is happening to me? Drunk? The Cognac Martin Bormann gave me. Drugged? Suzi, where are you? ... What day is it? It's Winter-time. Rudi-Winter-time. The tide is coming in, Father. Let me go, I'm going to drown like a rat. Like all your crew. Like rats in a submarine garbage scow... Don't leave me, Suzi. Don't let me drown in the Atlantic Reeperbahn. Don't—

"Wake up, Bach. Come on, wake up. You've slept long enough."

What time is it? "What? Oh. You!"

"Yes. Get up. Go take a shower. You'll feel better."

The last thing Dieter wanted to see awakening from a bad dream was Rudi Winter's face. *Had he slept in my room*? "A shower?"

"You're still half asleep. Get up. "I've already ordered breakfast sent up."

"You drugged me, didn't you?"

"Go get your bath. Then we can talk."

The old fashioned bathroom tile in rooms at the Frederik the Great have no rugs. The ice-cold tile on Dieter's bare feet jump-started his wakefulness, and the shower cleared most of the leftover nightmare cobwebs. He stayed in the shower longer than he normally would, trying to sort out what to do. The policeman had drugged him. Why? To make him easier to manage? *How did he get me into my room? Possibly the same way another taxi driver and I got Oskar up to his apartment.* Dieter dried off, wrapped a towel around himself and went back into the room. Rudi Winter was already sitting at the table eating.

The smell of food made Dieter nauseous, but he managed to dress himself and sit down across from him like a sullen schoolboy facing a headmaster.

"Coffee?"

"Is it drugged?"

Winter laughed. "I'm sorry about that. It was necessary for you not to make an unpleasant scene."

"How did you do it?"

Winter got up, went to the wardrobe, reached inside his overcoat and produced the silver flask, which he brought to the table. He unscrewed the cap and showed Dieter that there were actually two openings in its neck; one nearly normal, and one tiny one. "All I have to do is hold my finger over it, like this."

"Clever."

"Useful." He poured Dieter a cup of the coffee. "Go ahead, have some. I promise you it's straight."

In spite of his mood, the bitter coffee did taste good, but Dieter still had no appetite for any food. It was clear Winter had meant what he'd said about not letting him out of his sight. The instant that thought occurred to Dieter, immediately followed by the jolting memory of Winter's threat to kill him if he refused to give him what he wanted, he began thinking of some way to get away.

Winter chuckled again, not maliciously, but with obvious pleasure at being able to read Dieter's face so easily. "You can't escape me, Bach. Listen, I mean you no harm. Truly. Or your father. All either of you has to do is answer one simple question: You must tell me where your father is, or take me to him. Then he has to tell me where

Bormann and that gold is. After that, I will leave you both alone to get on with the rest of your lives."

At last Dieter found courage--or wit—enough to retaliate. "You won't do anything to me, Winter. If you murdered me, you'd never know where my father is, and you'd be right back where you started."

"Don't get smart, my naïve friend. I assure you I mean business. Last night I said I would kill you, and I would, but only after I hurt you very badly. And there are many ways to do that. For instance, what if your mother and your stepfather had a most unfortunate auto accident on that icy road into Freiburg? Don't think for a minute I couldn't make that happen. And poor old Oskar would have to go, too, because he's the only other link between us. Perhaps one night when he's drunker than usual, and falls down those three flights of steps at his place? Easy to break a neck like that. Then I could deal with you. Oh, you'll cooperate, all right."

"You wouldn't do that. You're bluffing."

Winter sighed, like a parent who has run out of calm logic with a stubborn child. He got up, stared at Dieter for a moment, then, faster than Dieter could have ever believed, sprang around behind him. With unbelievable strength, he jerked Dieter out of his chair, pinned both his arms behind him, and grabbed his right hand. Dieter felt Winter's fist close around his little finger, and heard it snap before he felt the pain. In the same motion, Winter dropped him back down in the chair. Dieter yelped, but it was nothing more than a fraction of a scream. "You broke my finger!"

His tormentor sat back down in his own chair as nonchalantly as if he'd merely stepped on an irritating cockroach. "And I will break another one each day you don't tell me what I want to know. Then I will start on more serious things."

The pain in Dieter's finger was sharp, but not as much as the pain in his head. The man *was* insane. A sadist. Willing to do anything to anybody. For the first time, Dieter began to believe Winter really could be the son of Martin Bormann.

"Who is Suzi?" The man's voice remained infuriatingly soft.

"What?" Dieter was immediately even more apprehensive than before.

"The girl, Suzi. You were talking some in your sleep. Who is she? Girlfriend?"

"One of many," Dieter lied.

"Must be a recent one. By the way, where did you go after you left the Mayo Clinic. I know you didn't go back to the Mayflower."

"California." This was only a partial lie.

"Yes, of course you did. You're a poor liar, Bach. Charlie is your father, isn't he?"

By this time the throbbing in his finger was acute, and Dieter barely heard his question. Winter must have then realized he would get little in the way of cohesive answers from Dieter while he was in pain. He got up again, went to the telephone and spoke to someone at the desk. Dieter could not hear all of what he said, something about first-aid. Winter hung up, turned, and poured two more cups of coffee, and lit a foul-smelling cigar. "I would offer you one, but I know you don't smoke."

Dieter glowered at him, holding his finger tightly. He couldn't believe how terribly it hurt, and it was already swelling. "You expect me to tell you where my father is, but I don't believe any of that nonsense about Nazi gold, or that Martin Bormann was aboard his submarine. According to what I read, there were several eye-witnesses who testified they saw Bormann's dead body in Berlin. Apparently, he didn't get very far after he left the bunker."

"They were mistaken," Winter said, talking through smoke rings. "The man you read about did escape. As I mentioned last night, he made his way, by a most circuitous route, and with the assistance of helpful Catholics, to Italy, where he lived in a monastery for a while, then dressed as a priest and with forged church papers cleared by the Vatican, made his way eventually to Argentina. This we know for fact. It's ironic that his legitimate son became a man of the cloth, don't you think? Perhaps that was the price the Holy Father demanded."

"You're contradicting yourself. How could he do all that and be on my father's U-boat at the same time?"

Winter leaned forward, enjoying himself. "Look, along with many others, I traced those leads for years, hot on the trail of that man from the Hitler bunker. I finally deduced I was chasing the wrong man. Only then did I start investigating other possibilities, military possibilities, which eventually led me to your father's records and to Trondheim."

"I still don't understand."

"Of course you don't. You see, I knew there were two of them. There were *two* Martin Bormanns. I had to locate both of them."

"Two? What the devil are you talking about?"

"Bormann had a twin. An actor who was part of the greatest double cross in the history of World War Two. You wouldn't believe how--"

A discreet knock on the door interrupted his narrative. Winter rose and admitted an elderly, anxious-faced bellhop carrying a first-aid kit. "Here you are, sir. Are you sure you don't need a doctor?"

"No, no," Winter said, taking the case and handing the old man a bill. "It's only a minor mishap. I can take care of it. Thank you very much."

The bellhop cast Dieter a nervous glance and left. Winter closed the door, brought the metal container to the table and opened it. From the contents inside he extracted a roll of adhesive tape, then rummaged around, grunting with displeasure. "Damn. What we really need is not here. We'll have to make do with something else." He shut the case, reached inside his coat pocket and brought out a pencil. "This will do nicely."

Dieter watched as he reached into his trouser pockets for a small pocketknife which he used to cut, then split the pencil down the middle. "What are you doing?"

"We need to set and splint your finger. Don't worry, I know what I'm doing. Here, give me your hand."

Dieter was sure the old bellhop--and half the hotel staff--heard his scream as Winter yanked hard on his finger, then held it while he placed the two parts of the pencil on both the top and bottom. "Hold this in place and keep your voice down. It can't be that bad."

Dieter bit down on his lower lip while the policeman quickly and expertly taped the improvised splint securely, then taped the little finger tight to his ring finger.

"That should do the trick," Winter said, with satisfaction. "Oh, I almost forgot." He reopened the first-aid kit, fished out a box of aspirin, shook two out, which he handed to Dieter. "Take these. The pain should die down shortly."

Dieter used the few minutes it took to go back into the bathroom for a glass of water to try to collect his wits. He felt both furious and grimly frustrated at not being able to think of some way to get away from this maniacal detective, and finally realized he needed to buy some time. Wait for some opportunity. He swallowed the aspirin, went back into the bedroom, and sat down across from Winter again.

Through the cigar smoke Winter grinned at him. "Are we all better, now?"

"I'll live. All right, Winter. I may be able to help you, but you have to admit this yarn of yours about all that gold, two Martin Bormanns, and all the rest of it is pretty fantastic. Unbelievable, really. Before I put my father into any kind of jeopardy, I'll have to see a lot more evidence that what you've told me is true. For all I know, you could be nothing more than some crazy guy with a long time grudge against my family. Show me some proof."

Winter eyed him for a full two of three minutes without making any reply. At last, he leaned forward and stubbed out his cigar. "As you wish. Actually, that is not an unreasonable request. I'm prepared to do just that, but first, you had better eat something. We have to catch a train, and it's a rather long trip."

Dieter felt a new wetness under his arms. "Train—? Where are we going?"

"To Munich." Then, with yet another of his good natured laughs, he said, "I'm going to introduce you to a movie star."

"A movie star?" Who?

"Edda Winter. My mother. Who, by the way, can supply all the proof you need."

No more than an hour later, they boarded a train for Munich, Dieter's mood black as Carolina tar, his splinted finger still aching, and his wrist bound to Winter's with handcuffs.

◆

Chapter 20

In Dieter's relatively short lifetime, he had become all too familiar with uninvited emotions of disappointment, embarrassment, grief, loss, and even despair, but until now, had never known the humiliating degradation and total subtraction of freedom endured by any common criminal. To be literally chained to a fixed piece of furniture or another human being who had complete control over him, whether inside a room or compartment, dining car, or even while using the toilet was nearly more than he could bear.

Worse, there was nothing he could do about it. Before boarding, Winter told him it would be not only foolish, but useless to attempt some kind of overt struggle or protest as soon as they were close to other people either in the station or on the train. He had already anticipated Dieter might scream out at the first person they saw that he was, in essence, being kidnapped.

"All I would have to do is show my I.D. and tell them you are a dangerous fugitive. If Germans respect anything at all, it's authority. I'm genuinely sorry I have to do this to you, but I can't gamble you won't bolt the first chance you get, plus, I have not had much sleep. Please try to understand, and don't forget the *quid pro quo* I promised," Winter said.

Dieter had swallowed two more aspirin tablets, but they hardly dulled the persistent ache in his finger-- which seemed to pick up the rhythm of the faint clacking of the muffled wheels. Usually, that sound—so persistent, so much like the steady playing of a good percussionist--would have been a little narcotic. Hypnotic. Like Ravel's *Bolero*, yet although his tethered abductor slept soundly, Dieter could not close his own eyes. After an hour or two, he decided the best thing to do about his predicament was to pretend to "surrender." No resistance. Be "resigned" to his fate. Play along with Winter until an opportunity came to get away. He still had plenty of cash in his billfold, as well as his credit cards, and it was not as though he was in a foreign country where he couldn't speak the language. Some chance would come. He was sure of it. So, he tried to relax, and to a small degree, he did, at least physically.

While Winter slept, Dieter studied his enemy, reassessing. Took new looks at his features. His clothes. Hands and neatly trimmed fingernails. Thought of how soft his handshake had been; so outwardly deceiving. The clothes, so ordinary, so off-the-rack plain, so obviously chosen to carefully hide a wrestler's body. Everything about the man; his voice, his demeanor, was subtly contrived to draw no attention to himself. To disguise enormous strength and superior intelligence. This was a person of formidable talents, and one whom it would be stupid—if not fatal—to underestimate. Dieter found himself speculating on how many men had. He shuddered and tried to think of something else.

Munich. Birthplace of the Nazi party. What was waiting for him there? For some totally unrelated reason, Dieter remembered one of the many stories Dr. Lert had told about Richard Strauss, his own mentor. How Strauss had openly sought the position of Reichminister of Music during the Hitler years, and when he succeeded in his ambition, refused to help former good friends and colleagues such as Bruno Walter to get out of Germany when things got bad for the Jews. And then, toward the end of the war, when the advancing American soldiers confiscated his Munich home, he rushed about complaining furiously, 'Don't you know who I am? I am Richard Strauss, composer of this and that masterpiece. You can't requisition my house!'

Naturally, those American G.I.'s, who knew Betty Grable, Mickey Mouse, K-rations and Kilroy, had no knowledge of *Der Rosenkavalier*, and had tossed him out on his impeccable ear. Lert had told how pathetically ironic it was that Strauss, left with no friends on either side, penniless, and completely depressed, wrote some of his most beautiful music before dying, a broken and pitiful man.

Munich. Home of the *Hofbrauhaus*, the famous *Oktoberfest*, fantastic beer, and still a hotbed of political activity. Where the *Putsch* and beer halls are as much a part of that city's life and history as the Yankees and Central Park are in New York.

Central Park and New York. His shooting. His career. All a million miles away. Centuries ago. His trip to Manteo. Suzi. Ancient history. Pea Island. Sunday. His father. Careful, Dieter, whatever you do, don't mention any of this out loud. Don't slip. Winter must not know. Concentrate on California.

He couldn't. He remembered reading Alma Mahler's book, which also described the extraordinary difficulties she and Franz Werfel had escaping Nazi Europe-- she, after escaping two disastrous marriages: To Gustav Mahler, who talked to trees and flowers, but not to her, and Gropius, who designed many of Hitler's favorite buildings before shrewdly abandoning his master's ship. And Alma lived in Lert's neighborhood! The kind of neighborhood Dieter had dreamed of for Suzi and himself. He found myself grinding his teeth from fresh anger and a new wave of self pity.

He then had an hour-long, painful vision of Suzi, which he tried his best to suppress, but could not, finally resorting to a little trick he had formerly used countless times during practice sessions that were less than satisfactory: He'd put his violin back in its case, lie down, close his eyes, and conjure up the most beautiful melody he could, using it as a nerve-calming device. Invariably, the same theme would seep, like osmosis, into his brain and psyche; the oboe's song which opens the second movement of the Brahms violin concerto, his favorite. Simple, pure, and exquisite, it was the best tranquilizer Dieter had ever found. But even Brahms' F-major love-child failed this time. He couldn't keep the smoldering ashes of fury tamped down. He felt like screaming, just for the release of it if nothing else.

He tried a different tack. .Forced himself to concentrate on details of their surroundings. The rich fabric and polished mahogany of the compartment. The recently dry-cleaned curtains draped at the large window. The small suitcases in the overhead rack. The leather handles of the traditional brief case every German businessman carries everywhere, like a religious icon. What was inside Winter's? What was his *quid pro quo?* What information could he possibly have that would make Dieter's life better?

At last, overloaded, his brain gave up. He must have fallen asleep, because whatever thoughts, conscious or unconscious, he was having were interrupted by the discreet three raps on the door, and a strong baritone on the other side of it saying, "Next stop—Munich main station, gentlemen."

In a kind of stupor, Dieter was led briskly from the train through the station, shoved into a taxi, and taken for at least half an hour's ride through the heart of Munich to a cluster of high rise apartments. They took open elevators to the fourth floor where Winter unlocked the door of apartment 408, and Dieter was gently pushed into the year of his birth; the year of Adolf Hitler's *Goetterdammerung.*

◆

Chapter 21

The small apartment was a museum. A shadowy shrine to German theater and film. Every wall was covered with framed billboards, posters, and more autographed photographs than in Sy's office. The surface of the mantel and every piece of furniture that had a flat top was cluttered with pictures and mementos, miniature kiosks, props and souvenirs from past decades of grandeur. And sitting in the midst of it all, like Cinderella in her ashes, was a thin, white-haired woman clad in a period dressing gown, smoking a cigarette which she held, Russian style, in a ridiculously long silver holder. She wore an unhealthy amount of powder and rouge, but her face had obviously once been beautiful. Her purple-painted lips parted into a tight smile that turned up slightly in one corner. She made no attempt to rise, although she did tilt forward, holding out a spotted hand for Dieter to bend over and kiss!

Her voice was like that of a small bird. Reed-like, but surprisingly resonant. "Ah yes, Rudi's violinist friend. Herr von Hellenbach, isn't it? Welcome to my house. Do have a seat, please."

She looked up sharply at her son. "For God's sake, Rudi, remove those nasty handcuffs. The poor man will think we're neo-Nazi deviates."

Winter freed Dieter from his manacles, and offered a glass of wine. "You'll be our guest here for only a day or two, answer a few questions for us, then I'll keep my promise to you." Altogether, his tone was friendly. Hospitable. As if to make Dieter feel comfortable in what was to be no less than a jail cell for two days. And a cell it was. He was fed a cold dinner, then shown the tiny guest room, which at least had access to an equally miniscule bathroom, but it would come as no surprise to Dieter that he was to be locked inside that night after listening to Edda Winter describe how she had met Martin Bormann, how she had become his mistress, and how she had learned of his incredible plan to double cross Hitler.

"Trouble was," she said at the end of her narrative, "The rascal double crossed everyone else, too, including me." She smiled at her son, and added, "He never knew about Rudi. After I left on that train from Berlin, I never heard from him again. He had given me quite a lot of money, but it was worthless within a couple months. We lost the war, you know."

"How did you and your mother manage?" Dieter asked.

"How would you think? Mother's looks were still good enough to hook enough of those generous G.I.'s for us to get by on until Rudi was born. After I got my figure back, we became a team. We were more popular than the Gabor sisters, by God, and spoke better English, too. We survived. When Germany was back on its feet, we both got character role work in the Bavarian Studios. My mother died two years ago."

Trying to maintain the feigned change of attitude he had decided on earlier, Dieter said, "I'm sorry you never got to Hollywood."

"Oh, I haven't given up on that old dream. It's what keeps me going. "I'll see it before I croak, especially if you're a good boy and cooperate with my son. He's really just a cream puff, and doesn't want to see you come to any harm."

Dieter looked at Martin Bormann's son, whose face was benign as his white shirt. "In Hamburg, you told me Oskar's story about the phantom submarine fitted in with facts you already knew. What were they?"

Winter shifted in his chair. "It took me ten years to trace and track down the surviving SS men who had served at that secret complex up at Trondheim, as well as the last routing of gold shipments my father had so ingeniously organized. It wasn't terribly difficult to track your father's movements, up to the time he was sent to Berlin. Doenitz himself told me about that. Then it was only a matter of simple deduction. Rather routine research of American and British naval records for the month of April, 1945 showed that no German U-Boat was sunk by any allied forces in the Atlantic during that month. As Mutti here told you, his secondary plan was to deposit the gold somewhere on the southeastern American coast, make his way inland with the captured American soldier to one of the P.O.W. camps, and wait out the war.

"It took me a long time to compile the names of repatriated German prisoners, but I had a good team working for me, and we managed to check them all. My father was not among them. I think his plan worked to perfection, and he's still over there somewhere. Get some sleep now. Tomorrow you'll tell me the missing piece of my puzzle, and we'll all be happy."

"All right, but do you have any more aspirin? My finger really hurts."

Winter stood, chuckling. "I've got something a lot better than aspirin." He walked over to the mantel, opened a small black case, and from it, extracted a hypodermic syringe. "Roll your sleeve up. I assure you this is a harmless painkiller, and will also help you sleep like a baby."

Dieter eyed the needle with renewed suspicion and fear. "What is it?"

"A muscle relaxant. Pentothal sodium."

It must have been a muscle relaxant, because all Dieter remembered after Winter gave him the shot was hearing gentle violin music and remnants of vague dreams in which he seemed to be telling his life story. He woke up again with yet another dry mouth, but hungrier than he'd ever been. When he looked at his watch, Dieter was not surprised that he'd slept almost twelve hours.

Edda and Rudi Winter fed him what they called breakfast, but with no coffee. Half an hour later, Dieter found out why. When Edda cleared the table, Winter brought in a large suitcase he blithely said was a portable polygraph machine. Apparently, he had not been totally satisfied with what he'd been told in the twilight of Dieter's drugged half sleep. He now wanted to test his captive while Dieter was fully conscious. Caffeine roaring through his system would not have helped. He soon had Dieter wired up and ready. “Relax, old friend, I’m an expert at this. What is your name?”

Dieter told him, and truthfully answered a number of insignificant questions while Edda looked on, a broad smile on her powdered face. Finally, Winter got down to the important things. “Is your father alive?

“Yes.”

“Where is he?”

“On Roanoke Island.”

“Has he told you of his last mission?”

“No, not in detail.”

“Do you know where my father is?”

“Yes.”

“Where? Is he also on Roanoke Island?”

“No. Your father is dead.”

“Are you certain of this?”

“Yes. The submarine was sunk by the Americans. My father was the only survivor.”

There was a long pause while Winter stared at the lines on the graph paper. Then, “Do you know where the gold is?”

“No.”

“Does your father know where the gold is?”

“I don’t know. I presume it was sunk with the submarine.”

“Did your father tell you anything about the gold?”

“No. He never mentioned it.”

“Do you know exactly where the U-Boat was sunk?”

“No.”

Again Winter paused in his questioning. Then, "Does your father know exactly where his boat was sunk?"

"I don't know. He was severely wounded."

Winter got up then, walked to the kitchen window and stared out, seemingly in deep thought. He stood there for several minutes until his mother punctured the pregnant silence. "I can't believe he's dead. All that work. Years and years of it. For nothing."

She also stood, and went over to him. Laid her head on his back. "This man's telling the truth. If that U-Boat went down with all that gold in it, how could we ever find it? And even if we could locate the spot, how could we salvage it? It's over, Rudi. All over."

Winter didn't answer her, and both seemed to have forgotten Dieter, who'd been holding his breath. After another few moments, Winter turned, gave Dieter a sort of embarrassed grin, and said, "I owe you a big apology." With those words, he came back to the table, disconnected all the sensors, packed the machine back into its box, and said, "Mutti is right, of course. You are telling the truth. Forgive me for doubting you, and for the regrettable inconvenience I've caused you."

"Am I free to go?"

"Yes. But before you do, allow me to keep my word. The exchange we discussed."

"I don't want anything from you except to get out of here."

"Don't speak too soon. You haven't seen what I have to show you." He left the kitchen, but came back a minute or two later carrying his briefcase. From it, he removed a manila file folder, which he handed over. “Take a look at that.”

Dieter opened the folio. Inside was a single photocopy of his birth certificate. He stared at it, then at Winter in bewilderment. “This? This is what you were offering me for my cooperation? This is something that is supposed to make my life better?”

Winter sighed. Take a look at the date.”

Dieter did. “June 1, 1945. So?”

“Now look at this.” Winter fished another file folder from his briefcase and handed it to Dieter. Inside were three documents, hand written and signed, neither of which made any sense to Dieter at all. “What are these supposed to be?”

“They are affidavits, sworn to and signed by a doctor and two nurses who assisted in your birth. Look at the dates again, von Hellenbach, and do the math. Your father left Trondheim on April fifth. Was your mother already seven months pregnant? I don’t think so.”

Dieter peered again at the three documents, this time reading them carefully, then, just as Winter had suggested, he *did* the math. The revelation hit him like a lighting bolt. Stunned and nearly sick to his stomach, he had to sit back down. “Is this... Is this true?”

“Positively. There can be no doubt. Shall we take the next train to Freiburg? It’s the least I can do for you.”

◆

Chapter 22

The handcuffs were no longer necessary on the train from Munich to Freiburg, but Dieter had completely forgotten about them. His broken finger was probably still aching, but he didn't notice it. His mind was far from clear, and his emotions were a strange mixture of new love and old hate, all of which he tried to unravel during the trip. Winter was helpful, to a degree. He said nothing at all, allowing Dieter all the mental privacy he needed in order to plan out the series of questions he needed to ask his mother and Harald. Anxious as he was for simple confirmation, Dieter most likely would have not given either one of them any chance to respond to them in depth before flying back to the States as fast as possible, but when he and Winter burst into their living room, Dieter's surprise was bigger than theirs: Like a smiling, muscle-bound Buddha, Oskar Knapp was sitting there with them!

It was his mother who spoke first. "Is it true? He's still alive?"

Dieter didn't answer her immediately. He looked at Winter, then at Oskar, and said, "Will you two excuse us for a few minutes?" Without waiting for a reply, he led his parents into Harald's study and shut the door.

When both were seated, Dieter looked at his mother, whose face was the color of three-day old snow. "Yes, it's true. Please, listen to me without interrupting. I don't have much time. I have to get back to the States as soon as possible. The short version of it all is, he was ordered by Hitler himself to undertake a secret mission to Argentina. They never made it. His boat was spotted and sunk near the coast of North Carolina, and he was the only survivor. One day, not too long from now, I'll fill you in on all the details, but in essence, that's it. He was rescued by a remarkable woman and has been living with her, more or less as man and wife, since April of 1945.

"I'm sorry, Mutti. I know you must be wondering why he never tried to come home, and it is nearly impossible to explain it, except that Germany as he knew it had ceased to exist, and that part of his life had died with all his shipmates."

Dieter didn't think it necessary to tell them the entire story. There would be time enough for that later. At that moment, his burning desire was to finish his business there and catch a train. The silence of their shock also helped. Like Winter, neither his mother nor Harald spoke a single word.

"However, before I go, there is one important matter to clear up. Stay here, please. I'll be right back." Dieter left them sitting there, walked back into the living room and asked Winter to give him the files from his briefcase. Winter handed them over with a smirk, and Dieter took a deep breath before going back into the study.

This time, he looked at Harald, trying to keep a neutral look on his face. "I owe you an enormous, life-long apology, and hope someday you will forgive me for all the unkind things I have thought and said about you."

"What are you talking about?" Harald said.

Dieter turned to face his mother. "What is my real birthday?"

"Wh... What?"

"My birth certificate says I was born on June first of 1945." He then glanced at Harald. "Your brother left her at Travemunde in April, but she was not pregnant then, was she?"

Harald stared at Dieter, then at the files in his hand, but never opened his mouth. "Let me see if I have this worked out correctly," Dieter said. "You made your way to Travemunde right after the war was over, didn't you? You brought Mutti back here to Freiburg a few weeks before you married her, in August."

Dieter handed him the three documents, and as Harald read them, he continued, "The date on your wedding photos was 15 August, 1945, and I was born on June first, sure enough, only it was not 1945, it was 1946! Horst von Hellenbach is not my biological father. You are. Why did you falsify my birth record? And why did you raise me as his son and not your own?"

The air in the study became like lead. Full of a heavy silence that lasted several minutes before his mother totally broke down. Between racking sobs, she tried to say something, but Dieter could not completely understand what it was; something about having no money, a war-widow's pension, considerably more if the widow was pregnant. She also blubbered something about getting the official notice of Horst's death at sea not more than a week after he had left.

There was no point in telling her that was also a part of Martin Bormann's plan. The unmarked U-Boat was never supposed to come back, and the letter she had gotten had probably been posted by his secretary.

"That's not the real reason, Dieter." Harald finally said.

Dieter turned back to him, eyes wide. "What was, then?"

"When she discovered she was pregnant, she refused to marry me unless we raised our child as his."

His wife shot him a glance of pure hatred.

"Forgive me, Elisabeth, but you know it's true," he went on, still looking at Dieter. "She wanted you to be a living memory of the famous war hero she had won and was to marry. You were to be her own Iron Cross with Diamonds. Her own fifteen minutes of fame, perpetuated the rest of her life by your very existence. I loved her, and was willing to do anything she wanted. At the time, while I was being de-nazified, I was not allowed to practice. We lived off the generosity of your grandmother, who had stashed away some long-exchanged dollars, and sold all her jewelry for more, God rest her soul. Later, it was relatively easy to change the hospital records. I have always been proud of you, Dieter, and what you have done with your life. This you must believe."

He handed the files back to his son, went over and put his arm around his wife's shaking shoulders, then looked back at Dieter. "It seems to me that if I could have forgiven her for that one selfish act, so long ago, you might also, although I daresay you probably despise her now even more than you have always despised me."

Dieter walked over to them and fell to his knees. "Oh, I do. I do forgive you. Both of you. You can't possibly imagine what a stone you have removed from my heart. I don't have the time right now, but I promise you I will come back soon and clear up a lot of things, and from this moment on, I will try very hard to show you how *happy* I am to be your son. I know you have no idea of what I am talking about, but you have freed me from a hell far worse than the one you have lived through for so long."

Harald nodded at Dieter. Then, as if he'd just thought of it, asked, "Who is that man you came here with?"

"His name is Winter. He's nobody important. Just a casual friend who has been rather helpful. I'll be leaving now. Will you two be all right?"

Harald stood. "Yes. We will be fine. When will we see you again?"

"I'm not sure. A few weeks, perhaps. Not more."

"Then, *auf wiedersehen*, Dieter."

He stuck out his manicured hand. Dieter grabbed it, then hugged him tightly--the first time he ever had. "*Wiedersehen... Vati.*"

Then came the thunderclap of shock from his mother, who hoarsely whispered, "He is not your son either, Harald."

For a long moment, time stood still. Dieter and Harald stared at her as if she had cut her own throat.

"When Horst left me there in that cottage, I somehow knew I would never see him again. I went to a local bar that very night. There I met a tall, very handsome former soldier who had lost a leg and was playing the piano there every night for a few tips and drinks. His playing wasn't bad, and I took him back to the cottage with me that same night. I slept with him every night from then until I was certain I was pregnant. I never even knew what his name was. I never wanted to know. After I was sure about my condition, that's when I wrote to you, Harald." When she finally lifted her head, she gave Dieter the saddest look he had ever seen. "I'm sorry, my son, but you have absolutely no von Hellenbach blood flowing through your veins. Harald is right about what he said, though. I wanted my own son to also be the son of a famous German hero. It was my vanity that has caused so much heartbreak. Please forgive me, both of you."

This revelation caused both Dieter and the Harald to momentarily freeze in place, like mute statues. When Harald von Hellenbach embraced his weeping wife, Dieter left them in the study, closing the door softly behind him. Oskar and Rudi Winter both stood. Dieter was sure they had heard everything. Winter said, "I took the liberty of using the telephone. A taxi should be here any minute. It seems we all three have trains to catch."

Still in somewhat of a daze, Dieter nodded. "What will you do now? Go chase more Nazi ghosts?"

Winter sighed. "No, not right away at least. I think I'll take my own mother on a vacation. We've never had one, you know. I've always wanted to visit the Greek Isles. You remember that coffee shop proprietor?"

"Oh, yes," Dieter answered, with a grimace. "I remember him well."

"He's from Crete. Used to talk about it all the time. I think my mother will love it there for a while. Then I suppose I will get back to work, as you say, chasing ghosts. I'm really sorry about your finger."

Dieter shrugged. "And I'm sorry you never found your pot of gold."

"What the hell are you two guys talking about?"

Oskar wanted to know.

"Nothing important," Winter said, "Just a clever figure of speech. *Ach,* here's our taxi."

All three of them stood in line and bought tickets, then shared beers at perhaps the same cafe table Bormann and his double had so many years ago; a coincidence Winter thought amusing. Dieter was wondering something else. "Oskar, you live in Hamburg. Why did you buy a ticket to Frankfurt?"

Oskar squirmed, then showed a sheepish grin. "Old Elke-the-Red don't pay me much, but I live cheap, and have managed to put a few D-Marks aside. If you have no objections, I'd like to fly back with you. I want to see him for myself. Sort of a reunion."

Dieter couldn't think of any possible reason to say no to that. It also occurred to him that Horst would probably enjoy seeing his old Chief again. "Why not? I think that's a fine idea."

Oskar's grin broadened. "Then you forgive me for... You know, for—"

"The thirty pieces of silver? Yes. I bear you no grudge, Oskar."

Winter laughed. "Don't worry, Knapp. Dieter here is full of forgiveness right now."

That was true. With what he had learned, Dieter was ready to forgive and forget everything and everybody. Even the men who had shot him! All he could think of was Suzi's face. And Sunday's. And her man Charlie's. Of their reactions when he told them—and showed them the documented proof of—the truth about his birth, and that now there was no reason at all he couldn't marry Suzi.

He was even forgiving enough to shake hands with Winter, whose train to Munich departed first, and noting with extended gratitude that the policeman was careful not to squeeze his taped finger too hard. Releasing Dieter's hand, Winter clucked. "You should have let the good doctor do that finger up properly while you were at home, but I think I understand your hurry. I'm guessing the reason you're so anxious to get back to U.S. is because of some woman there. One named Suzi? Am I wrong?"

"Good-bye, Winter," Dieter said, dryly, "I've told you quite enough about my private life."

"Indeed you have, Winter said. "Well, good-bye it is, then. We shall certainly follow your new career with interest. Let us know if you ever conduct in Munich."

"You'll be the first to know, Winter. My regards to your mother. Why are you grinning?"

"Can't help it. You and I are a certainly a polarized pair, aren't we? But with all that, we both have one thing in common."

"What do you mean?

"We are the innocent sons of our fathers. And *both* of us are bastards." Still chuckling, Winter turned and walked down the platform to his waiting train.

Their own train left half an hour later, and Dieter had forgotten Rudi Winter and his actress-mother before it reached Stuttgart.

◆

Chapter 23

"Would you believe?" Oskar said, "This is only the second time in my life I've flown in a plane. The first time was in a little Storch from Flensburg to Trondheim back in '45. Christ, what a difference. This thing's as big as the *Graf Spree!*"

Dieter had not paid any attention to which type of jet they were in. It may have been a DC-9. Whatever it was, Oskar was impressed. And grateful. In his own euphoria, Dieter had been generous to a fault back at Frankfurt; making up the difference in the price of converting Oskar's ticket to first class. He felt it was worth it, too, because watching the old submariner having so much fun--eating and drinking everything Lufthansa had stocked on board and flirting shamelessly with the amiable flight attendants--helped to partially contain his acute impatience. After a few hours, though, Oskar settled down some and went to sleep. Dieter briefly wondered what his dreams were like, and how much, if anything, Winter had told him of the real mission his revered Commander had undertaken.

Dieter also tried to sleep, and once more tried his Brahms trick— which failed again. He tried to get involved in the movie, but couldn't. Not even the good music available through the decent earphones reached his inner ear. He kept glancing at his watch, time after time, willing the jet to go faster. One of the very attractive attendants noticed his agitation and asked, "Are you all right, sir?"

Red-faced, Dieter told her he was. "Only a little nervous. I'm going home to get married." He was immediately struck by what he'd just said, especially that he'd referred to the United States as 'home!'

"Oh!" She said. "Why, that's wonderful. Then you must have some champagne. Best kind of medicine for that kind of condition!" Before Dieter could protest, she moved to her station and was back in a wink, a brimming glass in her hand and a smile of congratulations on her face. He took the glass, returned her smile and sipped, wondering if half the fuel tanks on commercial jetliners were full of booze. They never seemed to run out of it. Not on any flight he had ever taken, anyway. Amazingly enough, the champagne did relax him some, and he realized he was also hungry. The sandwich he asked for took the edge off, and he was soon dozing—

—And did not come fully awake again until they began their descent. Circling slowly over the busy harbor, around Ellis Island, and with the spires of Manhattan so close they could almost reach out and touch them, he commented, "Some sight, isn't it?"

Oskar had the window seat, his face plastered against the plexiglas, and Dieter felt a tinge of remorse that this aerial view was all the Big Apple tourism he was going to allow the former Chief, intending as he had to take the first available flight to Raleigh/Durham.

Oskar turned to respond, a misty look in his eyes. "I've been here before, son," he said softly. "Except I saw it all at night, through the lens of a periscope. That was in 1942. Your father—I mean, Lieutenant von Hellenbach, was the First Officer in that boat. Hadn't yet made his mark as a commander."

He paused to wipe his eyes with the back of his hand. "We raised a lot of hell up and down this coast before... *Ach*, never mind. That 'Good Time' was a long time ago. I'm looking forward to the one coming up." He glanced at Dieter and grinned as they felt the landing gear being lowered. "You suppose the Skipper of this boat knows how to dock her without scraping her gunwales?"

The skipper of the *DOLPHIN II* certainly knew how! Dieter and Oskar stood on the Wanchese dock as Sunday eased into her slip perfectly, her head and eyes plainly visible from the wheelhouse. Charlie, readying lines, did not at first recognize them; only that two fairly knowledgeable hands were offering to catch the bow and stern lines he tossed. Only when they were snubbed and cleated did he straighten, and then give Dieter a broad smile. Dieter watched his face undergo a drastic change when Charlie next took a closer look at his companion, who came to attention, saluted, then said, in German, "Permission to come aboard, Herr Kaleun? Got any grog on board this scow?"

Their reunion was a sight to behold. On the boring ride from Raleigh to Roanoke Island, Dieter had told Oskar of Charlie's injury, that his former Captain was unable to speak, and had to rely on Morse, or hand-written messages for communication. In turn, Oskar had haughtily replied that he had not forgotten all *his* Morse! There were nearly as many bear hugs as silent words exchanged between them that cold afternoon in the harbor at Wanchese. For his part, Dieter was grateful that Charlie and Sunday had already off-loaded their catch. Otherwise, Oskar Knapp would certainly have ruined what Dieter believed to be his only good suit and overcoat. As it was, it was more than an hour before Dieter was able to get in two words himself, and when he made his own astonishing announcement, producing the documentation that Winter had generously given him, along with his mother's long kept secret, not even Sunday had any objection to having alcoholic drinks passed around aboard her vessel.

Still, Dieter had no intention of extending such a joyous celebration without Suzi, who had not been aboard. "Where is she, Sunday?" he asked.

"She's in California."

"California?"

"Yes. With your teacher."

Dieter instantly lost his voice.

"We took her out with us after... After that night at Rosie's house, and she worked hard, too. We were at sea for over two weeks. When we got back, she gave up her trailer, packed one bag and left on her motorcycle. She called us from Raleigh. Said she'd sold her bike and was using her share of money from the catch to buy a plane ticket to Los Angeles. We haven't seen her since, but I have talked to her several times since then. She's fine. Got herself a job in a restaurant out there, and sort of keeps house for your Dr. Lert. I've got his number in our cabin. Why don't you call her?"

Dieter did make the call, but it was not Suzi who answered.

"Lert."

"Dr. Lert, it's Dieter Bach. I'm back in the States, and I have tremendous news. Is Suzi there?"

"No, she's working. What news?"

Dieter told him everything, running up the largest phone bill Sunday ever had, and then asked him not to say anything to Suzi. "If I can arrange flights, I'll be there sometime tomorrow night and tell her myself."

He hung up, made a few more calls for reservations, and announced to the others that he was treating them all to dinner at the Weeping Radish. Nobody ate much, however, and Dieter left the restaurant early, heading back to Rosie's house, finally exhausted from all the traveling. Plus, he knew he had more of it to do. He just didn't know how much . . .

Dieter couldn't believe how easily people could get married in California. Not even a blood test was required. In fact, a couple could buy a license and tie the knot as soon as they could find somebody authorized to do the job! All of this was just fine with him, naturally. Suzi, too. Half the morning after he'd arrived in Los Angeles was spent carefully relating to her--and again to his mentor--his whole macabre trip to Germany, leaving out none of the details. That very afternoon, they purchased a license, and were married the following day in a small Unitarian chapel in the Valley. Dr. Lert served as best man, his two sons their witnesses. The minister's good wife was a willing enough Matron of Honor, and before lunch, Dieter had a good wife of his own!

Dr. Lert took them out to dinner that night, and chuckled throughout the entire evening while Suzi and Dieter made hasty plans for a honeymoon. By noon the next day, Dieter had bought tickets for a week's cruise down the west coast of Mexico. (Suzi had already seen all she ever wanted to see in Hollywood and Disneyland, and was anxious to get away from Los Angeles.)

They were busy packing the new clothes they had bought when Lert knocked on his guest room door. "Dieter, you have a phone call."

Dieter's mind was not on telephone calls, so he gave no thought at all to who might be calling. He simply went to Lert's study and picked up. "Hello?"

"Dieter, this is Sunday. I'm afraid I have some terrible news. Charlie has had a massive stroke."

"What?"

"I'm sorry. I don't think he will last forty-eight hours, and he wants to see you before he dies. Can you come back right away? Now?"

Dieter's response was automatic. "Of course."

"Please. Come on the next available flight."

Sunday hung up then before Dieter could say another word. He put the phone down, and walked back into the guest room, his mind at that moment a total blank.

So, apparently, was his face. "Dieter?" Suzi said. "What's the matter? You look like you—"

"That was your mother calling. Your father has had a stroke. She asked me if I could-- Oh, my g*od!* What a fool I am. Idiot! *Idiot!"*

"Dieter, what the devil are you talking about?"

Dieter felt his knees give way. His legs wouldn't hold him up. He sat down on the edge of the bed, buried his face in his hands and tried to field the avalanche of thoughts that were descending on his brain. The first one, which had already crystallized, was how he had been duped. Lulled. "I've been *had.* Talk about double crosses!" he thought aloud, then, furious at himself for being so gullible, spewed out a stream of profanity that would have made any longshoreman proud. Suzi could only stare at him, still holding the blouse she had started to pack.

Dr. Lert came hurrying back to the guest room. "What's all this cursing about? What's wrong, Dieter? You're practically hyperventilating!"

Dieter's second clear thought became vocal. "Sit down, both of you." He looked at his new bride. "It's a damned setup! Suzi, your mother called *me*, not you. She told me Charlie has had a bad stroke, but I don't believe it. It's Winter. The bastard must have followed me to find out exactly where *Korvettenkapitan* Horst von Hellenbach has been hiding all these years. I'm sure he's there with your mother and father, and forced Sunday to call. Oskar Knapp must be in on it, too."

"What tipped you off?" Suzi wanted to know.

"Sunday's intelligence, that's what. By not calling here for you, and not mentioning your name to me was her way of telling us something was wrong there. Rudi Winter knows about you, but he doesn't know you are Charlie's and Sunday's daughter, and Sunday was obviously shrewd enough not to tell him. I never told him that, either. He's there, all right, and wants me back at Wanchese, too. He wants to know where that gold is and nothing's going to stop him from trying to get it. And, *if* he finds it, he's not about to leave any witnesses."

Lert said, "He's certainly a clever man. He knew all you wanted was to get back home to your Suzi, and you were so anxious to, and since you had truthfully told him that gold was at the bottom of the ocean, he led you to believe he had given up his search. It all makes logical sense." He looked at Suzi. "Dieter is right. Your mother and father are likely in great danger. You will be too, if you go back."

"Oh, we're both going back, Dr. Lert," Dieter said. "But I'm the only one they're going to see. Would you please call for a taxi?"

Dieter had crossed the Atlantic twice and traversed the United States four times within the last six weeks, but that final cross-country flight did not affect him in the least. His head was clear. Pulse even. Blood running through his veins like icewater. The flight gave him time to formulate a plan, pick it apart, refine it, pick it apart again, and then coach and drill Suzi on her part of it. By the time they landed at Raleigh/Durham and took a room for the night in a hotel near the airport, both knew exactly what each would do, plus a fall back plan in case they were fooled yet again. Dieter made the pre-planned phone calls, took Suzi down to the restaurant where they forced themselves to eat something, then back to their room where they went all over everything still one more time. Satisfied there was nothing else to do, they fell asleep in each other's arms.

Just as Dieter had expected, Oskar was waiting at the small airport at Manteo. Dieter managed to play his role well, acting the part of the shaken man who had—until a few days ago –been the only son of the dying 'stroke victim.' Oskar, to Dieter's surprise, also played his part admirably, saying over and over how sorry he was, and how much he felt cheated that his former commander had suffered such rotten luck just as they had begun making up for all those lost years. He sounded so *sincere*. Oskar had a rented car, which Dieter had also expected, and was glad to get in it right away. He didn't want to hang around that little airport very long, since Suzi would be no more than an hour behind him in a second chartered plane.

Oskar drove straight to Wanchese, parked the car, and led the way to Sunday's trawler. The moment they entered the main cabin, Dieter tried hard to show even more surprise. He must have succeeded, because Rudi Winter, who was leaning against the bulkhead, waved a silenced pistol toward Charlie and Sunday who were both sitting on the port-side settee, eyed him and said. "So, Herr Bach, you will forgive me for deceiving you one more time, won't you? As you can see, your former father is hale and hearty."

"Winter! What the hell is all this about? I told you the truth about the U-Boat and the gold. You said so yourself."

"So I did. You did tell me the truth-- as you knew it. Trouble is, except for knowing where 'Papa Charlie' here was, you didn't know what all the true facts *were*."

"I don't understand."

"You will." He motioned for Charlie to stand. "All right, Captain, up to the wheelhouse with you. Let's get underway, and don't forget, one wrong move, your nigger woman gets a bullet in her head. Oskar, cast off the lines, please."

Oskar went out on deck, threw the lines off, and as Charlie backed out of the slip, he pulled the fenders aboard. Within a few minutes, they were in the main channel, headed toward the inlet. Oskar came back below and sat down on the starboard settee. Dieter glanced underneath it. Suzi had told him Charlie kept his sea chest under the starboard sea berth. Sunday's was always beneath the port sea berth. And it was Charlie's chest Dieter was interested in. But he'd have to wait for the right moment. He turned to Winter. "Where's your mother? Did you leave her in Munich?"

Winter laughed. "No, no. She came with me. Probably still asleep at the hotel in Raleigh where I left her. Happy, too. She's half way to her destination." Dieter had no inkling what he was referring to, and said, "Where are we going?"

"Just out to sea a few miles, so we can all have ourselves a nice little family talk."

Dieter gave Sunday a hasty glance of encouragement. One she returned. He wondered if Winter knew how unafraid of him Sunday was. In any case, Bormann's son was not taking any chances. He kept the pistol pointed directly at her head. Oskar had not said a single word. Nor did he until *DOLPHIN II* was ten miles offshore. "I think we're far enough out, Winter."

"Fine. You go up and tell your old Captain to set the autopilot, then bring him down here."

Avoiding Dieter's eyes, as he had since he picked him up at the airport, Oskar did as he was told. Two minutes later, he returned with Charlie, whose face showed only consummate contempt for his old Chief and his kidnapper.

"Do have a seat, Captain, and let's get down to brass tacks." Winter looked at Dieter. "I might as well fill you in on the fascinating facts you're unaware of. First, I told you the truth, more or less, about my father's double. He was an actor. A friend of my mother's, and must have been a terrific one, otherwise old Bormann would have never trusted him to do what he did. I neglected to tell you that I actually did go to South America, practically on the heels of the Israeli squad that snatched Eichmann. Eventually, though it was not easy, I met the man most professionals think is Martin Bormann.

"True to his profession, he continues to 'act' out various roles and personalities, disguising himself expertly, and moving around from place to place like the hunted animal he really is. He might have fooled me, too, but gave himself away when I told him how Bormann had double-crossed him along with everyone else. Nevertheless, he did have a money source, and I suspect the other Odessa fugitives, believing he really is Bormann, have helped him financially."

Winter paused long enough to ask Oskar to look in the refrigerator for something to drink. Without waiting for him to come back with it, he went on, this time looking at Charlie. "It took me a long time, and some of the best police work I had ever done, to locate the one man who held the last piece of the puzzle. With the written guarantee of immunity I gave him, Otto Skorzeny told me of his detachment of SS commandos who loaded the gold onto the U-Boat, and were aboard when she sailed. By the way, I knew that none of them had ever returned to Germany, so I deduced that Bormann's plan had worked. Skorzeny told me half the torpedoes aboard held the gold, and half held enough explosives to destroy a small city. The timing device was in the Commander's cabin, which Bormann was to take for himself. This tally with what you knew so far, von Hellenbach?"

Charlie nodded, hate and sorrow mixed shining through his pale blue eyes.

Oskar had found Charlie's beer, and handed Winter one. He sipped and frowned. "American beer! Tasteless. Well, anyway, the reason I know the gold did not go down with the ship, as they say, is that my father would never have blown the U-Boat up until it had been off loaded. Skorzeny confirmed that. No one was to survive except himself and his companion."

"Who was that?" Dieter asked.

For the first time, Sunday spoke. "A small man with a money belt around his waist."

Winter inclined his head in her direction. "That would have been Corporal Bobby Joe Reams. An American flyer who was, for that much money, willing to take my father inland to Williamston. His object? To infiltrate the Prisoner of War camp there, bribe whomever necessary, and wait out the rest of the war. All this I know from my mother."

He stopped his narrative long enough to order Oskar to check on deck for traffic, then said, “Bormann had only one weakness. He talked in his sleep!” He glanced at Dieter. “Jabbered more than you did under the penathol. My mother didn’t know everything he did, naturally, but between what I learned from her, what the actor told me, plus the information I got from Oskar and Skorzeny, I’ve been able to put it all together, except for one last thing.”

He stood, walked over to where Sunday and Charlie sat, stuck the pistol to Sunday’s nose, and said. “One or both of you know where that gold is. I’m certain my father hid it before he blew the boat up. I know he did that, because he was the only one who knew where the detonator was. The gold didn’t sink with that boat. He would never have allowed that to happen. Now, that strip of beach back there is several kilometers long. Where exactly did he bury it?”

Dieter interrupted just as Oskar came back down, giving Winter an all-clear signal. “What if you do find it?”

Winter turned to him and shook his head. “I’m surprised at you, Bach. You’re a reasonably intelligent man. Our good *Korvettenkapitan* here surely hasn’t forgotten all his navigation skills. I’m positive he can steer this vessel first to the Cayman Islands, then to Mexico. There, we can all live like kings, wouldn’t you think?”

Sunday looked him dead in the eye. “He won’t do it.”

Winter lowered the pistol, and with his left hand, gave her a vicious backhand slap across the face, bringing a trickle of blood from her nose. “Oh, yes he will. Otherwise, you will lose your extraordinary good looks, gradually and painfully, and then you will die before his eyes. If you don't believe me, ask Dieter. Now, my patience is waning. Where is the gold, and what happened to my father?"

Dieter's rescue plan was rapidly disintegrating. He broke in. "He *means* it, Sunday. For God's sake, tell him where it is if you know."

Sunday wiped the blood from her nose. "They buried the gold around my house on Pea Island, but Charlie and I moved it. As for your father, if that's who it was, I killed him. I drowned him and cut his ugly throat."

Winter stared at her. "So the double-crossing son of a bitch is really dead? Well! Serves him right, but I don't give a shit. Where's the gold now?"

"You're standing on it," Sunday said.

"What do you mean?"

Sunday pointed straight down.

Oskar came to life. "She means below decks. It's here, in this boat!"

Sunday nodded, then gave Charlie a pleading look. Charlie stood, motioned for Oskar to follow him, and then walked through the cabin toward aft, toward the engine room. Five minutes later, both returned, each carrying what looked like a large, black brick. Oskar's face was one broad smile. "It's down there, Winter, in the bilge. This boat has some ballast! Look here." He placed the brick on the deck, took out a pocketknife and scraped the top. The black paint came off easily, revealing its true color.

A dead silence came over all of them. Winter took a few steps backwards, leaned up against the bulkhead again, and reverently whispered, "Finally." After a few moments, he looked at Charlie. "Are you ready to set a course south?"

Charlie glanced once at Sunday, then at Winter. He shook his head in the negative. Sunday, in a panic, immediately jumped up. “I can navigate just as good as he can. I’ll take you wherever you want to go.”

“I can help, Winter,” Oskar volunteered. I ain’t forgot all my seamanship.”

Winter nodded at both of them. “All right, then, let’s get moving. We can probably make some port in South Carolina or Georgia before we have to refuel. I hereby charter this boat for a fishing expedition to Mexico, by way of Grand Cayman.”

Dieter never would have believed Charlie could move so fast. In practically one motion, he wheeled around and by the time Winter--or anyone else—reacted, he had reached the door to the wheelhouse, grabbed a loaded flare gun from its designated niche, aimed and fired straight at Winter’s head. Had he had aimed at Winter’s body, he might have succeeded, but the flare missed by inches and smashed against the bulkhead like a starburst, singeing the back of Winter’s head and setting fire to the curtains closed over the portholes. Everyone was momentarily blinded, but Winter was the first to recover. He took two steps toward Charlie, raised his gun and fired twice, knocking Charlie backwards. Sunday screamed as her husband crumpled to the deck, landing on his back. Winter, with no more pity than his father must have had, then pointed his pistol at Charlie’s forehead and fired a third time. Then he turned, aimed the gun at Sunday and yelled, “You want to be next?”

Sunday stood mute, her entire body shaking with fury.

"Get up to that wheelhouse and get us underway," Winter said. "Now!"

Sunday gave Dieter a look of total helplessness, turned, and obeyed the command.

Winter then gave Oskar an order. "Strip his body and throw it overboard. Then find a mop and clean up that mess."

Oskar must not have heard him. He was staring at the body of his beloved commander with tears in his eyes.

"Did you hear me, Knapp?"

Oskar turned to face him. "I heard you. You promised me there would be no killing. Damn you to hell and perdition, Winter. You can shoot me if you want to, but I'll be god-damned if I throw him overboard like a rotten side of beef. I'll find some canvas and bury him decent."

Winter's face seemed to soften a bit, no doubt because he knew he would need Oskar's help in managing the trawler. He nodded. "All right, do it whichever way you want to, but get it done right away. The less his woman sees of this, the better off we'll all be."

An alternative plan came to Dieter in that instant. "Wait, Oskar, Charlie kept his old uniform in the chest under this berth. Let's dress him in it for his burial. It's the least we could do."

Oskar looked at Dieter with a new kind of respect, and then glanced at Winter, as if asking for his approval. Winter was rubbing the back of his burned head, obviously in some pain. He shrugged. "Fine. Just get on with it."

Dieter's heart rate climbed as he pulled the trunk from beneath the bunk, turning it so that its lid faced

Winter. To distract Oskar, he said, "Thirty pieces of silver and now thirty pieces of gold. Are you satisfied finally?"

Oskar ignored him and started undressing his former Captain, sobbing uncontrollably. Dieter began throwing piece after piece of clothing from the trunk, feeling for the loaded pistol he knew was there. The moment he felt it cold in his hand, he eased it aside and removed Charlie's uniform, which he handed to Oskar. When the battered, filthy white cap came out, it was the final straw for the former Chief. He fingered it for a moment, then emitted a roar like that of a wounded bull, then stood, and charged Winter much the same as that bull might have charged his tormenting matador. Dieter closed fingers around the handle of the old Luger, praying it was still operable.

Two shots into Oskar's chest didn't even slow him down. His momentum crashed Winter against the bulkhead and they both went down in a writhing heap. Another shot came. Then yet another. Dieter saw Oskar's huge body twitch even as he raised Charlie's weapon in his own good hand. Winter, rising up on his knees, shoving Oskar's body aside, saw it and tried to free his gun arm from underneath Oskar's bulk He succeeded, but not quite in time. Dieter closed his eyes and pulled the trigger. Once, twice, a third time, then again and again until all he could hear was metallic clicking. When he opened his eyes, he saw Sunday standing in the passageway, a sawed-off shotgun in her hands, her eyes wide with surprise.

Winter's eyes were wide as well, but they would never see anything in this world again. Dieter was not sure how many of his shots hit the bulkhead or how many may have hit Oskar's body, but some of them had found his intended target, and it was all over. He had no idea of how long he remained sitting there next to Charlie's body. The rest of his shock-filled actions were a blur; helping Sunday clean up, dragging Oskar and Winter out on deck, removing a hatch cover, and dumping them into the fish hold.

He was vaguely conscious of helping Sunday finish undressing Charlie, then dressing his bloody body in his old uniform, and he remembered watching Sunday sew it up in some canvas—with both the gold bricks to weigh it down, and he was definitely cognizant of how hard it was to lift Horst's body and lie it down on top of his berth.

He then followed Sunday up to the wheelhouse, watching her change course and speed up, and may have told her that Suzi had been trailing them in the sportfisherman. It may have been the temporary deafness from the shots of Charlie's pistol still ringing in his oversensitive ears or it may have been that he simply paid no attention to Sunday when she called Suzi on the VHF radio.

He didn't know how long it took for them all to reach the spot Sunday steered to, but he did know when she stopped the boat, shut down the engines, and left the wheelhouse to go below decks. It was only much later he'd remember that she had opened all the seacocks, and had poured diesel fuel all over the exterior of the boat. The cold water of the Atlantic jolted him into enough awareness to realize he and Sunday were floating in it, then climbing aboard Charlie's charter boat and seeing Suzi's relieved face. He turned and watched with awe as *BLACK*

DOLPHIN II burned and sank, carrying *Korvettenkapitan* Horst von Hellenbach and his Chief Engineer down to join their mates; a veritable Viking's funeral, complete with a dead dog at their feet, and with nearly enough gold to buy their way out of hell.

Sunday tried to tell Dieter he hadn't killed Oskar Knapp. "I'm sure he was already dead before you began shooting, Dieter. You must believe that." Dieter tried to, but failed.

Largely because of Sunday's wide reputation, the maritime inquiry into the loss of her boat was blessedly short. She and Dieter simply testified they had been hijacked by some unknown foreigners looking for a treasure-salvage ship, there had been a fight, a fire, and they had been lucky to escape with their lives. The whole thing had lasted only part of two days, but Dieter, still in a state of shock, had hardly been aware of the brief formal proceedings.

Sy's news that the Fort Lauderdale Symphony wanted Dieter to replace their departing Music Director should have pulled him at least part way out of his newest depression, but it didn't, even after an interview there which Dieter went through in a mental fog, with Sy doing most of the talking.

His and Suzi's belated honeymoon at Orkney Springs the following summer should have been another rung on the ladder of his climb out of his hell-pit, but he'd done so badly even Lert was embarrassed for him. And, his first couple of concerts at Ft. Lauderdale had been less than brilliant, to say the least, and after the third one, with his concentration so obviously lacking, half the audience had left at intermission, and that night, Dieter had a complete breakdown.

◆

Chapter 24

New York. January 3, 1982

Her beauty turned heads of both sexes as she strode purposefully from the elevator down the corridor and through the open door of Glazer Artists, Inc. Without a word to anyone, Susan Bach marched right past both the surprised receptionist and a furious secretary, threw open the door and walked into the private office of Seymour Glazer. No one had noticed the ordinary shopping bag she carried, or that she was several months pregnant.

From behind his messy desk, Sy looked up, hung up the phone and with his other hand motioned for his secretary to retreat, then stood. "Susan! Good to see you. Please, won't you have a seat?"

"Only for a minute," she said, her voice as cool as the outside air she'd brought in. "I've come to bring you this."

The package she removed from the shopping bag and handed him was a manuscript. Dozens of bound legal pads filled with handwriting he immediately recognized, also noting that the first page was in the form of a letter.

Sy sat back down, removed his glasses, shifted his considerable bulk sideways in his chair, and looked up over the neat penmanship at the face of the very pregnant woman he had once begged Dieter not to marry. "You sure you want me to read this, Susan?"

"I'm sure. You are his oldest friend. Maybe his only friend, besides me, I mean. I think he wrote it for you anyway. It was your idea in the first place, remember?"

Sy nodded, lifting the six-inch thick stack of paper from his desk, weighing it. "This must be a thousand... A whole book!"

"I know. It took him this whole year to write it."

Sy puffed his cheeks out. "Yeah. Okay, I'll read it, even if I already know what's in it."

"You don't know half of what's in it."

Sy grunted, surprised and rebuked. To disguise his discomfort, he replaced his glasses and dropped his eyes back down to the first page of Dieter's manuscript:

Sy,

I am addressing this to you since you are likely the only person who will ever read it. You will find some redundancy, and for that I apologize. However, you will also learn of long kept secrets. Nazi secrets, along with Sunday's and Charlie's, which I expect you to be no less amazed to discover than I was. I urge you to keep all this to yourself, as I have.

This writing, from memory and diary notes, has been my way of dealing with all that has happened. And, I have learned to cope with the fact that I have blood on my hands. But I do not apologize for killing that pig. Not in the least. Nor for what

> Sunday and I did with the gold. I believe it made a fitting gravestone. Don't judge me until you read everything.
>
> Dieter

Sy looked up again, this time sharply. "Killing? Gold? What gold? What's he talking about?"

All he got for an answer was a shrug. He knew Susan had never liked him. Blamed him for a lot of what had happened, which was absurd. He sighed and nodded again, closing his eyes. Susan's silence was her way of making sure he'd have to read the whole thing. So be it. But what was all this about gold? Dieter and Susan's mother had done something with some gold. "Have you read this yourself?"

"Sure I have," Susan said. "Every single word." She stood abruptly, and placed a key on Sy's desk.

"What's this for?"

"You'll know after you've read it all. I'm leaving."

"Where are you going?"

"Home to have my baby."

"You serious? There's nothing left down there."

"Mama is, and it's still home. We'll be better off there than anywhere else."

Before Sy could respond, she was through the door. Gone. He knew better than to chase after her, offer her money, or even a ride to the airport. No, not the airport. She'd walk to Grand Central and take a train. A lot like her mother, Susan was.

Sy leaned back in the huge leather chair, thinking he'd wait until tonight to start reading. Then, he leaned forward again, staring again at the opening page of the diary manuscript. *Apologize for killing that pig...Nor for what Sunday and I did with the gold. . .*

The sentence seemed to jump off the page at him. Dieter had never mentioned anything to him about any gold, and for damn sure had never said anything about any killing! What the devil was he referring to? In any case, his office was no place to concentrate on Dieter's writing. There would be fifty phone calls before he could read a dozen pages. Sy had other artists and their careers to worry about besides Dieter's. He pursed his lips, calculating. It was Friday afternoon. He'd take the rest of the day off and spend the entire weekend reading, certain it would take that long to read the thick manuscript. Besides, he was curious as hell about the gold mentioned on the very first page, not to mention what Susan had said about his not knowing half of what was in the diary. What on earth could he not know about Dieter Bach? He believed he knew every facet of the man's extraordinary life. The triumphs. The tragedies. The resurrection of his life and career. Susan's words had sounded ominous as well as sarcastic. What the devil was *in* this book? What Nazi secrets could Dieter be alluding to?

He rose from his desk, stuffed the manuscript into his briefcase, and was reaching for his coat when he had a second thought. On impulse, he punched the intercom button. Betty Friedman, his overworked secretary answered instantly, "Yes sir?"

"Betty, pull the Dieter Bach file. I'll pick it up on my way out."

"The whole file?"

"Yeah, all of it. I'm going to take it home with me."

"You're going home?"

"Yep. Glazer Artists can run itself one half a day without me."

"I wouldn't bet on it."

"I'll chance it. And Betty, hold all calls and messages till Monday. I don't want any interruptions."

"You're the boss, boss."

Sy frowned, dropped the key Susan had given him into the top desk drawer, grabbed his coat and left the office, clutching the heavy briefcase to his chest like a new-born baby. An hour and a half later, he was in the living room of his Brooklyn Heights townhouse, Dieter's manuscript on his lap.

For once in his life, he wasn't hungry, and shed tears as he read the first few pages:

This purge, written from diary notes and painful memory, is an accounting of the string of events after I was mugged that October night by Central Park. While none of it will mean much to anyone outside my small circle of friends and family, it may someday make sense to my audience, should I ever have one again. And that is what I pray will eventually happen.

I have a fine place in which to work; my mother's cottage just north of Travemunde. It's bitter cold here on the Baltic. So different from the warm shores I have left behind, yet I have established an exercise routine here similar to what I had there. Like every good German, I walk. Each morning before I sit down to write, I walk, no matter what the weather. (It's usually too foggy to tell.) Here, fog is palpable, and holds me in a moving padded cell, like the way the quilted numbness of guilt had straight-jacketed my brain for the past several months.

On the beach, it's much too raw for long walks, so I force myself to go along slowly. Good for reawakening emotions. Occasionally, the fog drifts faster than I do, allowing me to glimpse the plodding Baltic rollers, the rough shell beach, and the frigid sky, all melded in grays and muted blues, like Lionel Feininger's shadings, totally devoid of real color or warmth.

But whether it is clear or not, and no matter how many layers of wool I have cocooned myself in, when I return from these contemplative walks, I feel as though my body and brain has been enshrouded in layers of liquid ice, and I'm enormously grateful for the sight of the stone steps that lead up to the cottage— and the promise of Suzi's coffee, which also warms the fingers of my right hand enough to hold a pencil. I'll get used to this exile I suppose, as I have the cottage, which is as ugly as the indigenous terrain it was carved out of (I have nicknamed it Quasimodo!)

Suzi, of course, is a wonder. She moves silently around the four rooms, either ahead of or behind her own shadow, depending on where the light is coming from, reserving sparse conversation to mealtimes, then she goes to bed early, leaving me to my tapes. Every night, after writing more in this narrative, I listen to two hours of repertoire, programming them into my memory bank, hopefully to be withdrawn later.

Last night, Suzi said we should have a child. That being a father would help me through all of this faster. I am not so sure. The thought of becoming a father has never been a single link in my thought chain, but then, I had never once given any thought to dying either. When one is young, such a morbid thought would never occur. But on that October night in New York, half a block down from the Mayflower, I knew I was going to die. My life was going to be over the next instant.

Yet, I was given a reprieve. Granted a second life. Will I be lucky enough to have a third one? Maybe Suzi was right, after all . . .

It took Sy three days and nights and several readings before he could believe the incredible story in Dieter's manuscript. He was engrossed in the closing letter when he finally heard the persistent banging on his door. He cursed softly, laid the final pages down on top of the empty pizza boxes stacked on his coffee table, and walked to the door to see who the intruder was.

Betty Friedman was standing there on the stoop, in snow up to her ankles. "I was about ready to call the police, already! Have you gone nuts? It's *Tuesday*, for God's sake. Have you forgotten you have a business to run?"

"Come in, Betty. I'm sorry. I should have called."

Betty used her umbrella to knock the snow off her feet, and walked past him into a scene that caused her another anxiety attack. "Oh-my-God! Look at this room! Sy, what in hell have you been *doing*? This place looks like the bottom of a dumpster!"

"I guess I've sort of neglected to clean up recently. What are you doing here, Betty? I told you—"

"Listen to me, Seymour Glazer, I've worked for you eighteen years now, and most of the time I can run the agency as well as you, but the reason I came here is to tell you that your son has been sitting in my office for two days."

"Robby? Why?"

"He's dropped out of school again. This time he wants to go into business with you. He wants a job, Sy."

"No kidding?"

"Would I kid you about something like that? Admit it. You've been hoping for that ever since the kid was twelve."

Betty took another disgusted look around the living room. "*Jee*-sus. This place is the pits! Now, couple things: You take a cab, if you can find one running in this weather, and get back to the office. Then I want you to take Robert with you and go on down to Washington early. Take the time to show Robert some of the ropes. While you're gone, I'm gonna get a professional cleaning crew in this pigsty, and when you get back from Dieter's concert, you gotta make some tough decisions. What's kept you holed up in here so long anyway?"

Sy retrieved Dieter's last pages. "Betty, let me read you something."

Betty crossed her arms. "So read."

Sy put his glassed back on and read part of Dieter's closing letter:

. . .purge, my purgatory, was actually over two months ago, Sy. I have been working hard on my concert repertoire for Washington since then, and you'll be pleased to hear that I feel great about it. I know you stuck your own neck out getting me that concert, and there is no way I'll let you down. Or myself. I only hope that the baby doesn't come before I get back from my talks with the good people at Ft. Lauderdale. I'd really like to be back on Roanoke Island for that occasion.

One last thing. Suzi will give you a key. I found it in an envelope in Charlie's trunk. The envelope was addressed to me, along with a note that said to look in the Trailways Bus Station at Elizabeth City. If you get to Roanoke before I get back from Florida, will you please go there and see what it unlocks?

Also, please consider being my child's Godfather. Nothing in the world would please me more.

Again, my thanks for all you have done for me, especially the suggestion to write this whole nightmare out, which has, as you guessed, freed my soul.

Dieter

"Touching," Betty said. "Can I read the whole thing? After we get this place cleaned up, I mean."

"Sure, Betty. What tough decisions were you talking about a minute ago?"

"Decisions concerning *me*, you blind jerk. Next time you see me, you got two choices: Either fire me or marry me. Better still, fire me *and* marry me. I'm your only hope and you know it. Otherwise, you're gonna catch bubonic plague or something worse living like this."

She grinned at him, grabbed his head between her hands, and kissed him lightly on the lips. "So call a taxi, you fat-ass slob, and let me get to work."

◆

Chapter 25

Sy and Robert spent several delightful father-and-son days together, first in Sy's office, then in Washington, and by the time Dieter's concert on January twelfth came around, Sy was convinced his Robby was truly serious about following in his footsteps in the business. He also had another thing to be happy about. Aside from developing the belated relationship with his son, he was also convinced he had possibly overlooked a perfect mate for eighteen years, and could hardly wait to get back to New York.

As for Dieter, if he was disappointed that Susan was unable to attend because the baby had not yet arrived, he didn't show it. He was in a zone, and the concert itself was, as Sy had prayed for, a huge triumph. A smash. Along with Robby, he'd sat in Rostaprovitch's private box at the Kennedy Center, feeling the electricity build, measure by measure, and before the last majestic notes of the Shostakovitch Fifth had died away, was on his feet along with the rest of the packed house, shouting "Bravo" after "Bravo."

Dieter took several curtain calls; the orchestra applauding as much as the audience. Sy nudged his son. "Bet you a C-note he gets offered a return engagement."

"No bet. What's he going to do next?"

"He's going back down to Ft. Lauderdale and take up where he left off. He's on his way, Robby. Come on, let's go backstage, and then we'll see if we can find a decent place to eat in this town. My guess is all the reviews will be raves."

They were. Because of the joyous post-concert celebration, none of them got much sleep that night, and were really dragging when they said their good-byes the following morning at Washington National. The rotten weather had nearly caused their limo to be late, so they shook hands hurriedly, promised to be in touch, and parted company; Dieter to Ft. Lauderdale before going back to Manteo, Sy and Robert to catch the shuttle back to New York.

Totally bushed, Sy arrived back at his Brooklyn Heights townhouse around dinner time, and would have been astounded at its transformation had he not first spotted Betty sitting in front of the television set, bawling her eyes out. It took Sy some two or three minutes to realize what she was watching. Through the dense snow falling in front of the news cameras, the scene was surreal; the tail section sticking out of the ice and water, the police, the lights, the mayhem. Sy sat down on the floor, put his arm around Betty, and caught the gist of what the news anchor was saying:

Air Florida flight 90
Hour and a half delay
De-icing
Runway 36
Crashed into the 14th Street bridge

Hit seven vehicles
Potomac River ice-water
Dieter's flight.

They didn't see that Dieter Bach was among the first of the seventy-four passengers rescued; dragged from the icy water before any permanent damage could be done.

Thinking Dieter had been one of the many fatalities, Betty whispered, "What will you do?"

Sy wiped fresh tears from his eyes. "Long term, I don't know. Short term, I have to go south again. Dieter asked me to be the child's Godfather."

"I'm going with you."

"No. You stay here and help Robby with office stuff. This is something I have to do alone."

"Any idea how long you'll be gone?"

"As long as it takes, Betty. As long as it takes."

◆

Epilogue

In July of the summer of 1999, Sy and Betty Glazer sweated buckets while watching Robby's two daughters romping on the beach, their father constantly herding them away from the water's edge. "Robby and Barbara have their hands full with those two," Betty said.

"Fact," Sy agreed. "The kids and Barbara are having a helluva good vacation, even if Robby isn't. He's worse than I ever was. Can't wait to get back to the office."

"Me, I can't wait to get back to some air conditioning at the hotel. I swear, it's hotter here than it is in Naples."

"Yep, that's another fact. Well, soon as Barbara gets her pictures, we can drive back. I think I could drink ten beers."

Betty gave him a sharp glance. "You'd better not have so much as one, lover. Your heart wouldn't take—oh, here she comes."

Sy turned his head to the left. His long-legged daughter-in-law, cameras strung professionally around her neck, her face tanned nut-brown beneath a straw hat the size of the Bronx, was striding toward them, her lips stretched into a Julia Roberts grin. "Got 'em," she said.

"Amazing. Two little gray gravestones sticking up in all this sand. Great composition."

With a grunt, she plopped down beside them. "You know, Sy, I'm really glad you talked us into this trip. Watching them move the Hatteras lighthouse was interesting. Some piece of engineering. I got some good shots, which I should be able to sell somewhere, but these shots on Pea Island are better. Tell you what, I don't think I ever really believed that old story until I saw those two headstones and that pile of rubble you said was once a house. One thing you never did tell us, though. What about the key? What was it for?"

Sy scowled. Looked out over the surf. Didn't answer.

Betty punched him in the side. "Oh, for God's sake, Sy, tell her. It won't matter after all these years. They wouldn't mind. Not now."

Sy waited another few seconds, and sighed deeply. "Okay, I'll tell you about it, but not out here. Let's see if we can get the kids back to the car. I'm dying in this heat."

He waited until the air in Robby's SUV made driving bearable, and said, "Dieter was one of the first ones pulled from the crash. As you all know, he had some frostbite, but no serious or lasting damage. Thank God, he had survived yet again. That was the main thing.

"While he was in the hospital, I drove over to Elizabeth City, mostly from curiosity. Went to the bus station. The key fit a locker there. Only thing in it was an envelope with a handwritten note inside, in Charlie's handwriting."

"What did it say? Barbara asked. "Can you remember it?"

"Word for word: *'Yellow sunlight lies at the feet of A.G. Bell amidst the snow peas.'"*

"Pretty poetic," Barbara said.

"Pretty cryptic," Robby added.

"Took me a while to figure it out," Sy admitted.

"But you did."

"Sure. A.G. Bell had to be Alexander Graham Bell. His 'feet' were obviously telephone poles. Poles 'amidst the snow peas' on Pea Island. Plenty of them still grow there. Anyway, at night, all by myself, I started digging around the base of every damn telephone pole from one end of the island to the other. Found nothing. Zilch. Until it finally dawned on me I was looking in the wrong place."

"I don't get it," Barbara said.

"I had forgotten that some years ago, they had moved the road we're on. It's now several hundred feet further inland than it was back then. All I had to do, once I had that figured out, was to locate the spots where the original poles had been. Didn't take me more than a week. Hardest physical work I ever did in my whole life."

"And?"

"I dug up six ingots of gold, that's what. Old Charlie had provided for one heck of a rainy day. Can you believe? Sunday didn't even know about it. The State of North Carolina took half, but I still had enough left for what I needed to do."

"Let me guess," Barbara said. "Sunday and her daughter."

"And her grandchild," Robby put in.

"You got it. I sold my house in Manteo to Sunday for one dollar, and helped her get another boat. Except for those two headstones you photographed back there, the rest went into trust for the kid."

"You're a good man, Seymour Glazer," Betty said.

"Ain't I though? Anyway, that's what the key was for. Charlie had figured Sunday might need it someday."

Barbara whistled softly. "Wow! And all this time I thought you had financed the whole nine yards yourself. So, what's next?"

"We'd all best get some sleep tonight. We've got a long drive ahead of us tomorrow."

With all the pit stops they had to make between Nags Head and Winston Salem, their trip took the whole day. By the time they settled into their rooms at the Holiday Inn, the children barely had enough time for a quick dip in the pool before dinner, and Barbara was just a tiny bit miffed that there was not enough daylight left for her to run over to Old Salem and get some shots of the Moravian village. "No matter," she said, "I can do that tomorrow, guys. I'll stay here with the kids at the pool. You go on over to the recital."

Sy frowned at Betty. Both knew that Barbara, talented as she was, had tunnel vision regarding music. Her tastes ran from Rock to Roll. Period. They showered, dressed, and met Robby in the lobby. "Ready?" he asked.

"Ready," Sy replied. "I've been waiting for this a long time. Ever since I retired."

The recital hall of the prestigious North Carolina School of the Arts was packed– in spite of such an odd time of year for such an event. The Steinway on the otherwise bare stage gleamed like a polished Rolls, and on the front row facing it, Sy easily recognized Susan and her mother, and though he could see only the backs of their heads, knew they were dressed to the nines, and grinning from Atlantic to Pacific. Between them sat a man with a gray ponytail and wearing sunglasses.

Sy, Robby, and Betty joined in the applause as the pianist strode confidently onstage and took his first bow. Sy leaned over and whispered to his wife, "Robby's new meal ticket!"

Charles Sontag sat down and reached long fingers to the keyboard. Tall, handsome as hell, with a mane of curly black hair, and with stage presence the likes of which Sy hadn't seen in thirty years, the boy played Scarlatti, Mozart, and Debussy flawlessly, and with astonishing maturity. Not another sound invaded the auditorium. Not one rattle of a program. Not one single cough. Sy found himself holding his breath.

At intermission, he stood with Betty and his son, who were already in animated conversation:

"Terrific!"

"Sure fire Cliburn winner in a year or two."

"Best prospect since Andre Michel Shub."

"Looks and charisma to burn."

"Lead pipe cinch. Can't miss."

Sy nodded. He took a step toward Robby. "You bring that contract with you?"

Robby beamed, and patted his jacket pocket. "Got it right here, Pop."

Betty nudged Sy. "The son of his father, for sure." She inclined her head toward the auditorium. "Him, too. Funny about it, though. Why won't he use his full name?"

"I should think that's fairly obvious, Betty. He was named after Charlie and Sunday—that's the Sontag part, in German. He doesn't want to cash in on his father's name. Wants to make it on his own."

"Well, his Dad made it here just in time, didn't he?"

"Oh, yeah. Dieter wouldn't have missed this for all the gold in—never mind. Looks great, too doesn't he?"

"He does that," Betty agreed. And nobody has recognized him yet."

"And probably won't. Not until it's over. Hey, lights are blinking. We'd best get back in."

The second half of the recital; three exquisite Rachmanninoff Preludes followed by a thundering performance of Shubert's "Wanderer" Fantasy brought down the house. The audience brought the young pianist back for a dozen curtain calls, but Charles Sontag played only one rousing encore; one of his own compositions: "Variations on a Southern Folk Song."

Sy doubted if many in the hall recognized the tune, even though the words were printed at the bottom of the program:

Old Dan Tucker was a fine old man
Washed his face in a frying pan
Combed his hair with a wagon wheel
And died with a toothache in his heel

After his son's final bow, Dieter Bach glanced backwards over his shoulder, caught Sy's eye and smiled. Sy winked back

Having noticed the exchange, Betty leaned over and whispered, "Wouldn't it be wonderful if the boy could make his debut with his father?"

Sy waited for a second or two before responding. "I think Robby's working on that already. At least he'd better be, if he's any son of mine."

Contented, Sy closed his eyes, thinking of another couple of lines—all he remembered of a little poem he had learned a hundred years ago at school.

God's in His heaven
All's right with the world.

◆

About the Author

A Tarheel native and son of amateur musicians and writers, Tom Lewis was born in Rocky Mount, North Carolina, graduated from New Bern High School, and was further educated in the United States and Europe. Before retiring to seriously write for publication, Tom spent 38 years as a symphony orchestra conductor in Europe as well as Charlotte, NC, Roswell, NM, Rochester, MN, Tulsa, OK, and Sioux City, IA.

In addition to his trilogy, Pea Island Gold, he has written five other novels, a collection of short stories, and one book of non-fiction. Tom currently resides in New Bern, NC.

Also by Tom Lewis
Lucifer's Children

In the eternal struggle between the forces of good and evil, twin protagonists try to thwart Lucifer in one of his myriad plans--to recruit converts from all walks of life by means of a diabolical baby farm; tempting innocent souls with wealth, romance, eternal youth, and other grandiose lies. The hero and heroine (twins) are at first not even known to each other. One, MAGGIE ELLIS (a TV anchor) and RAMON BARILLAS (a Catholic priest) stubbornly fight Lucifer tooth and nail through many hardships and tribulations, and at great cost, until a final dramatic climax that has Good triumphing over Evil--for the moment. Come along with Maggie, Ramon, and a strong cast of unforgettable characters in this fast paced tale of horror, electrifying action, and incredible suspense, set primarily in the rugged, austere mountains between North Carolina and Tennessee. Let Tom Lewis take you along on this amazing journey, where along the way you will find characters you will love, some you will despise, and ultimately discover whether you can sleep, or keep from turning the next page!

Printed in the United States
137399LV00005B/32/P

9 781607 670018